Right
Solution

# TITLES BY JAY GEE HEATH

*Romantic mystery*
Right Talents
Right Skills
Right Dreams

*Mystery with romance*
Right Response
Right Target

Tiger's Adventures in the Everglades
as told by T F Gato, a cat with attitude
Tiger's Adventures in the Everglades volume 2
Tiger's Adventures in the Everglades volume 3

ISBN eBook 978-0-9992454-5-3
ISBN Print Book 978-0-9992454-4-6
Library of Congress Control Number: 2020922637
Naples, Florida

# Right Solution

jay gee heath

# DEDICATION

*As always*

*Sam*

I want to acknowledge here that I have stretched the truth in the interests of telling the story. I took liberties with the FBI and the sheriff's department locations and titles.

The Rock and Grant insisted I should include a section on shuffleboard so if you don't like the hats blame them.

Thanks to
Janet Benjamins
Jean Smith
Jo Anne Sullivan

# MONDAY

Cav grit his teeth, braced himself, then took a sip of the coffee. A small sip. He was tough. He was a cop. Been a cop for fifteen years and the stories about cop coffee were all true. He knew bad coffee. And Lori's coffee? It went way beyond bad. The first sip was always the worst because she could make bad in a wide variety of ways. It might be weak, colored water, which would at least be drinkable. Or it might be flavored. Peppermint once. But chances were, it would be thick and dark. Bitter. Often with grounds. Well, always with grounds. How did she do it?

He swallowed. Didn't grimace because the coffee this morning was good. And his dilemma this morning wasn't the coffee. It was Lori. She had something on her mind. Something which had been bothering her. Something he was afraid he wasn't going to like. He'd caught her a few times, tongue caught between her lips, watching him with a thoughtful look. Each time she'd begun to say something, then stopped and turned and walked away. He hadn't asked her what was wrong. He was a cop. He knew the signs and they weren't good. She was giving off all the dumping-this-guy vibes. Today, he thought. Today, she's going to dump me.

He'd given her time to find her own way, he didn't want to hear her say the words. But he'd only been putting off the bad news.

1

It was time to man up. He took a second sip of coffee. Still good. Maybe it was an omen.

He leaned against the counter, affecting a casualness he didn't feel, he sucked in his gut and asked, "What's wrong?"

She stopped spreading the strawberry jelly on her peanut butter, peanut butter she'd made by mixing dry peanut powder with cream cheese, and turned to him.

Except she looked at his tie, she didn't look at him.

Not good.

"I, ah, I think I have a problem with, um…" She stopped.

He waited, holding his breath.

"I think I have a problem at work."

Whew. At work. Not him. He almost smiled in relief, but she was visibly upset, her hands fluttering. She didn't seem to know what to do with them, waving the jelly knife. This nervous, restless person wasn't the woman he knew and loved. Nothing upset Lori.

How could she have problem at work? And why would it involve him?

He waited. But she turned back to her sandwich.

He walked three steps to her, took her by the shoulders, and sat her down in a chair. Poured her a cup of coffee, set it in front of her, and sat kitty-cornered to her, knees almost touching.

"A problem at work. Tell me about it."

She popped right up again, waved her arm, walked around the kitchen, a full circuit. Again.

He waited.

She sat. Finally said, "It's kind of weird."

"Tell me."

She looked him in the face this time and took a deep breath, "Mrs. M? My patient at the retirement center?" She stopped.

"Yes," he said, "Mrs. M, the lady with the tax jokes." Because whenever Lori said 'Mrs. M? The tax accountant?' she would tell him a funny tidbit or an odd tax statistic. Seemed an oxymoron to Cav. Witty tax accountant?

Lori was a physical therapist, and Mrs. M was her patient. They had become friends during the therapy sessions and still visited together now that the woman was recovered. Lori called her Mrs. M because she couldn't tell him her patient's name or condition because HIPAA, the Health Insurance Portability and Accountability Act, rules required data privacy and had security provisions for safeguarding medical information. So, an alias—'Also known as Mrs. M'. He wondered if Lori ever thought of it that way.

Lori stuck her tongue between her lips. Took a breath. "Last week she said she was thinking of selling her house. You know the one. The little blue house on Dolan Street?"

He nodded. He did know the house. In fact, lusted after it. "Yes. White picket fence, gingerbread trim." Pretty little house, off the main drag. He frequently went a block out of his way to drive by and look at it. It had been empty for a few months and he was hoping to see a "for sale" sign on it. Had even asked Kevin to keep an eye out. But then he saw people had moved in, and he'd been disappointed.

"Yes. Well, Mrs. M has settled into the Forest Retirement Center and she's happy there with all the amenities. And she's made lots of friends. She's in a conundrum, her word. She thinks she should sell. Or maybe rent it." Lori stood and went back to her sandwich.

Cav's ears perked up. He voted for selling.

"If she rents," Lori continued, "she'll need a property manager. Right now, her neighbor keeps an eye on it."

"Okay." He waited, because Lori was talking as if the house was still empty.

"Well, Mrs. M? She told me her house is empty. Closed up since her accident."

Huh? He shook his head. "No. It's not. A young couple with a baby moved in three weeks ago. Mrs. M is old. She's confused."

Lori glared at him. "She is old and has a physical problem. Not a mental one. She's not confused or forgetful. She says the house is empty." Her voice had an edge to it.

"Okay. Okay." He tried again. "Maybe when she was in the hospital, on drugs, she changed her mind. Decided to rent. And forgot."

"I thought of that; she was very sick. And her attorney could possibly have decided on his own to rent the property, because it's always better for a home to be occupied. Right?" She shook her head. "Mrs. M just doesn't make that type of mistake."

She put down the jelly knife with a clatter and closed the jar.

He gave her a sympathetic look. "Honey. If you're worried, why not suggest Mrs. M contact her attorney?"

"I don't want to upset her." Lori looked at her sandwich. Sat down. Took a sip of her coffee. Grimaced. "Cold."

He took it away and poured her a fresh one. Waited for her to get to the problem. He was sure there was more.

She did the tongue between the lips again. Looked over at him. "Last week she invited me for tea with her two new best friends, Mr. K and Mrs. Tubalt, The conversation turned to homes. Both own houses and are in the same position as Mrs. M, happy at Forest and ready to make it their permanent residence. Should they keep their homes for a sense of security or acknowledge it's time to move on this new path and enjoy retirement at Forest and sell. So sell or rent their homes. It's a big decision."

He nodded, poured himself some more of that excellent coffee. "And now they're thinking they like where they are and don't need to be tied down to real estate. Got it." He had no idea where this was going.

"Mr. K, the farmer, another client. You might remember; he's the one who used that phrase, 'Katy bar the door'?"

She waited for him to acknowledge he knew who she was talking about. With a smile, he said, "Something funny always happened after Mr. K said that." Guess folks in a retirement center needed humor.

"Right. Anyhow, Mr. K said, *'Katy bar the door, Max. We'll be neighbors.'* Then he patted her hand and told her his place had been vacant over a year, and he was still undecided about selling, though maybe it was time for someone else to make it a farm again." Lori stopped, took a sip of her coffee.

Not done yet, Cav decided. She still hadn't gotten to the problem. He made a guess. "Sounds like there may be some hanky-panky at the retirement home. Is that what's bothering you?" He didn't think so; Lori would be happy for the couple. Not troubled.

She stood and walked back to the counter. "No. I think it's sweet." She put the peanut butter and jelly away and sat down. "The third person at tea, Mrs. Tubalt, is a friend of both Mrs. M and Mr. K, but she isn't a client. She's an ex parochial schoolteacher and principal. She's awesome. Small, diminutive, always wears matching tops and pants. I suppose there are stores which must sell them. And she collects buttons. She says she can carry all her treasures in two boxes.

"Anyhow, she's lived in the retirement community for two years and hasn't sold her home because it's her only physical tie to her husband. It's where they lived together for thirty-five years. She has a property management company."

Lori looked him in the eye. Now she was getting to it, he thought.

"The thing is. I took a ride out there, to their homes. The farmhouse looks abandoned."

He pulled his hair. "You said he doesn't live there anymore. No one lives there. It should look abandoned, honey."

"No. Not empty. Abandoned. The yard is overgrown, the windows boarded up. Flowers dead."

"So, he has a bad caretaker. Probably a neighbor."

She frowned. "Maybe. I didn't drive up to the house, only

parked on the roadside. The thing is, I could hear rumbling, like an engine running."

"Mower? Or Air conditioning. Keep the house at an average temperature," he suggested.

"Not from the yard. Or the house. The barn. The engine sound was coming from the barn. And a car was half parked behind it. A black Jag." She took a breath. "It didn't feel right. Felt creepy. Something about it." She looked down. "I was scared. Silly, I know."

His cop senses tingled. Scared. Was her gut telling her something was wrong? You always listen to your gut. He tugged his hair, started to speak, but she held up her hand. "Wait. There's more."

Lori stood and paced. He frowned. It was unlike her to be so fidgety.

"I took a drive to Mrs. T's after I went to the farm. I missed it the first time, so I made a U-turn and came back. I missed it the first time because the car in front of me, a green clunker, turned into her driveway. When I came back, I saw a different car come out. I pulled to the side of the road and double-checked the number. It was her house. I couldn't see it because it's hidden down a long driveway and behind trees. The green beater came out while I was sitting there checking the address."

She sat again. "The house is supposed to be empty, closed. There shouldn't be any vehicles going in or out."

"Maybe the caretaker." But he didn't like the sound of it, and that must have shown on his face.

"You think it's something, don't you?" she said hopefully. "I'm not imagining things?"

"It does sound curious. Why don't you give me those addresses and I'll go take a look."

"You don't mind? It's Saturday."

"I'm working."

She jumped up, back to her normal, decisive self. She opened her daily journal where she kept hard copies of patient information.

Her appointments she kept in her cell. She sifted through the pages and then hesitated.

"I'm not sure. I don't think this is violating patient confidentiality. It's just addresses. But what happens if you find something criminal? I've told you some personal medical information about two of these people. It was okay when I didn't identify them, but now? Now you'll know where they live and who they are."

He gave it some thought, because it was a serious issue and he wanted to put her at ease.

"If it doesn't turn into anything, I'll never know their names; I'll never meet them. No breach of rules or ethics. If you have uncovered a crime, you didn't tell me anything I won't learn when I interview them. It would all come out then. Either way, you're okay." He walked over to her. "Give. And I'll swing by and take a look. Put your mind at ease." And his, too.

She searched his face. Decided he couldn't help if she didn't share. "Okay. Thanks. I was afraid you would laugh at me and tell me I'm imagining things." She gave him the addresses, thought about her other problem. Her personal problem. With him. But she wasn't ready to go there yet. She wanted more time to consider what her next step would be with Cav. Wasn't ready to discuss it. Besides, she'd just saddled him with enough. She finished putting her sandwich together. Sliced it, wrapped it and put it in her lunchbox, a soft sided thing with butterflies on it. Added cookies and zipped it up. Threw it over her shoulder. Picked up her leopard to-go cup. By that time, she was ready to give him her happy, I've got no troubles in the world smile and a quick kiss. "Call me? Let me know?"

He kissed her back, relieved she wasn't dumping him, instead had given him an interesting mystery. "Sure," he said, "anything else?" Because something was still there. But she was out the door. Seemingly, back to normal. Decisive energy in motion. He smiled, shook his head. Love that woman.

The thought gave him pause. He'd used the *l* word. He considered it. Mouthed it. Love. Repeated the phrase. Love that woman. Hah. Love? Him? Shook his head again. Drank some more coffee.

Deal with it later. Best get to work and stop daydreaming. He didn't like the sound of three supposedly vacant homes being occupied. One maybe. It happened. Even two. But the coincidence that three of the residents in the same facility had the same problem? He didn't like it. He picked up his cell and called Jones.

"We have a side trip to make. Wear casual street clothes, jeans. I'll pick you up in half an hour."

Next, he called his secretary to let her know they'd be in the field most of the morning. Then he went to change out of his uniform.

They headed for the Estates home first, it was the closest. The homes were built on five acre lots and most were set back, hidden from the street by trees and shrubbery. People liked their privacy. Cav had spent some time on Google maps to familiarize himself with the area before he left Lori's. He drove past Mrs. Tubalt's drive and turned into the driveway one lot down across the street, drove up to the turnaround in front of the house, and came back and parked diagonally across from Tubalt's mailbox, number 2185.

"What are we looking for?" Jones asked.

"Watch and see." Cav turned on some country music. Tapped his fingers on the steering wheel in time with the beat. Waited. Shouldn't be long.

About ten minutes later, a brown Dodge Charger came out, no mufflers. Cav snapped pictures of the vehicle, adjusted the long lens, got the driver, then the tag.

"Run the tag," Cav said.

Jones called in the number. "No wants. Owned by a 'L. S. Corp'. We could stop him. For the mufflers."

"Let's not do that yet. Watch some more."

Fifteen minutes later a black Avalon came slowly down the road, turned into 2185. After ten minutes, the black Avalon left. Cav shot pictures of the car and driver. Jones ran the tag. Another half hour, a black SUV drove slowly past. Pulled in at the last house on the dead-end street, backed out, drove back, and turned into 2185.

"Out of state," Jones said.

Cav snapped more pictures; Jones ran the tag. They repeated the process two more times in the next hour.

"No one's staying very long," Jones pointed out. "Only long enough to drop off something or pick up something else. Not white slavery. Drugs would be my guess. A stash house."

Cav didn't let his smile show. The kid was good. Had good instincts. Was fast becoming his best cop. A little more seasoning on the streets, he would make a good detective. "Could be a home business. Selling on Amazon, Etsy, Craigslist."

"Oh. Hadn't thought of that," Jones said with a trace of disappointment.

"Doubt it, though," Cav added.

"Out of state mean something?" Jones asked.

"Means whatever is going on here crosses state lines," Cav replied, nodding to himself. Yup. Good cop. He'd caught the significance of the tags.

"Too bad we can't see the house. Want me to hike through the woods?" Jones asked.

Cav had given that some thought earlier. "No. I expect they will have some sort of warning system. Guards."

All the tags came back with some type of minor traffic violations, but no warrants. The two waited another forty-five minutes, but no other vehicle came or went.

Cav pulled out and headed west, out of town, to the farmhouse. The land was open here. A long straight two-lane highway bordered on both sides by small family farms. Old white houses near the road, barns behind or beside. Not many trees, mostly pastures with cattle or fields of corn. White picket fences, barbed wire. He parked across the street from the farmhouse. Possibly in the same spot Lori had stopped. They could see Mr. K's house and barn.

"Grab that oil can from the back seat and go raise the hood."

Jones gave him a frown but did as he was told.

The house did look abandoned. The windows halfheartedly covered with plywood. The yard unkempt. The Jag was parked in front of the barn today. No attempt to hide it. The vehicle didn't fit; farmers don't drive shiny Jags.

He snapped pictures of everything. No way to get the tag number, though.

He watched Jones lift the hood, set the oil can on a bracket by the engine and fiddle with some wires. Took his hat off and scratched his head. Wiped his forehead, while he looked around. Turned back to the engine. Upended the oil can as if pouring. Fiddled with some more wires. Closed the hood. Came back and got in the truck.

"Hear anything?" Cav asked.

Jones closed his eyes thinking. "Tick-ticking from the hot engine. Bird singing in that tree." He pointed. "A/C going strong. Non-stop. Not cycling. That's it."

Cav was silent, considering.

Jones said, "Don't know much about engines, but this truck was running fine. So, what are we doing here? No traffic in or out. Quiet. Except for the A/C. Is that it? Is that what we're looking for? Listening for? You're always asking me what do I see? What do I hear? What do I think it means?"

Cav waited.

"Okay," Jones continued. "No activity here. The Jag doesn't fit. Expensive car. Machinery running. Sounds like a lot of power being used and it's being used in the barn. Not the house. If the place in the Estates was a sell house, the barn could be a meth lab."

Cav nodded. Proud. "Possible. Remind me about that cold case you solved. You're in court with it next week, right?"

"Methamphetamine lab explosion, last year. The building was a foreclosure located in the middle of a wilderness tract and was supposed to be vacant. There were some car and truck tire imprints, but no type of vehicle was identified. Becca had me run the treads because most treads are now in the system, and she thought I might get lucky. And she suggested I walk around the area, re-interview the neighbors."

Becca had been mentoring Jones at the time. Mentoring Jones because she was bored while recuperating after being shot on the job. Recuperating at her brother Kevin's gatehouse where she'd lived while finishing school. Recuperating and exercising with her therapist Lori, Jones sister. Full circle.

Jones continued, "I found a woman who had been up north at the time of the explosion and was never interviewed. She said she saw the son of the former owner hanging around the place with his buddies. She thought that was strange, but never connected it to the explosion. I checked DMV; found he was still driving the same truck. The tires were the same type as the treads I'd run. Confronted him and he confessed."

Jones looked over to Cav. "That's when you asked the banks to keep you informed of foreclosures and abandoned homes. Is that what these are?"

"Not quite. We have one more."

He started the engine and headed back to town and parked down the street from the little blue house. Not so little. Colonial, two story, with a hip roof. Two chimneys. Gingerbread trim. Two sets of windows either side of the front door, matching windows upstairs. Windows sparkly and clean. Porch across the front of the house with a glider, rocking chairs, and hanging plants. Two car garage, door open. Small sedan, out of state tag. Oh, yeah, definitely occupied.

Pretty house. Friendly. Happy. He really did lust after it. He pointed. "That house is said to be vacant."

They both watched a woman watering the hanging plants. A small child playing with a truck on the deck.

"It's not. Unless, she's just visiting. Watering plants," Jones said.

"I've seen her and the kid three or four times the past couple of weeks. A man too."

"You think they're homesteading? Squatting?" Jones asked doubtfully.

"I'd sort of like to know the answer to that," Cav admitted. Gave Jones a *what are you going to do about it* look.

Took Jones a minute to get it. "Oh. Right." He reached for the door.

Cav warned, "You're a private citizen. Not a cop."

"Right. Got it." Jones stepped out and ambled up the walk to the house they were parked near. Climbed up on the porch and rang the bell. Waited a few moments and rang it again. When there was no answer, he tried knocking. Peered in the window. Looked around and seemed to notice the woman next door. Stepped off the porch and walked over to the next yard.

"Excuse me, Ma'am," he said in his best imitation of a country boy, tipping his head and touching his hat.

She'd been watching him. "Yes?"

"I'm trying to find Miss Emma Lou Rawls. My Granny asked me to look her up. I've been trying to reach her by phone for a couple of days with no luck and decided to come by. Do you know when she'll be home?"

Cav could hear him. Good play. The kid was good. Cav would have believed the aw-shucks country boy act.

The woman frowned. "We're new to the neighborhood. I haven't met Miss Emma Lou. What a quaint name. Seems like I've seen an older lady in the yard. And a younger guy. Does that sound like her?"

"Oh. She'd be an old lady, but Granny Iris didn't mention that anyone lived with her." He had a puzzled expression. "You haven't met Miss Emma? That doesn't sound like her. She would have brought you some of her famous brownies when you moved in."

The woman shook her head. "We haven't really moved in. This is temporary housing for us."

"Still, the minute she saw the moving van, she'd have been over." He managed to look worried now.

"We didn't have a moving van. Our things are in storage."

"You buy this place furnished? Excuse me Ma'am. That is none of my business. I didn't mean to pry."

She laughed. "Oh, we didn't buy. Our builder arranged for us to stay here while he gets the occupancy permit for our house. Some glitch in the system has the county a few weeks behind schedule. They keep saying tomorrow and I'm reminded of that story where tomorrow never comes. Though this is a pretty nice house to be stuck in."

Jones nodded. "Still. Miss Emma should have been over. Though maybe, if your builder puts people up here, she's used to the comings and goings."

"I don't know. Jeffrey said he lucked into this house. The only furnished place in the area."

"Jeffrey? Your husband?"

"No. Our builder, Jeffrey Newton. He doesn't make a practice of running late on his contracts. He came with really good references."

"I'm sure. Should have introduced myself. I'm Andy Jones. That's my brother in the truck."

She held out her hand to shake. "Peggy French. My son Jason." She had a firm clasp, shook and stepped back.

"Pretty place. Granny Iris seemed to think Miss Emma Lou lived in a duplex."

"No duplexes on Dolan Street."

"Dolan Street? Wow. My brother must have typed the wrong street name into the GPS. I'll have to razz him about that." He motioned to the truck. "No wonder I can't find Miss Emma Lou. She's on Donlan Street. Don't know what to say, ma'am. Sure feel

silly. But it was a pleasure to talk with you. You have a nice day now."
He tipped his hat.

"Not a problem. Except now you've made me hungry for
brownies."

They both laughed and he headed back to the truck where Cav
was just packing up the camera.

Jones got into the truck and sat. "Didn't get much. You hear?"

"Yeah. Interesting. Thoughts?"

"Questions first."

"Okay."

"This place is supposed to be vacant. All three properties supposed to be vacant?"

"Yup."

"All have the same owner?"

"Nope."

"In foreclosure?"

Cav almost shrugged. He had the foreclosure problem eighty-five
percent sewed up. Because of Jones's cold case, his office called each
bank every Friday for a list of foreclosures and abandoned property.
A few of the banks called them. Either way it was labor intensive
for the clerks. The lists were combined and passed out at roll call. A
car went by each property two or three times each shift. That kept
squatters out.

It cost money for banks to maintain foreclosed properties and
sometimes they were reluctant to spend the money. Cav's office
encouraged the banks to keep the properties in good repair which
also discouraged squatters. Return on investment would be larger if
the properties were in good condition. And it made the neighbors
happy.

But buildings which were abandoned during pre-foreclosure were
another matter, there was no way to track those. Or the voluntary
vacates. And then there were the fifteen percent of homes not mort-
gaged to banks. He'd thought he was ahead of the problem with

the foreclosures, but apparently the crooks were still leading, because these homes didn't fall into that category.

"Not foreclosed."

Jones thought some more. Then said, "Very different properties. Different locations. Different enterprises. One in a quiet residential neighborhood of small families. This woman was friendly, and I didn't sense anything off about her. Comes across as innocent. If anything is screwy here, maybe the builder?"

Cav motioned for him to continue.

"The Estates place. Isolated. Off the main drag. Private. As much traffic as there was, the quick turnaround, my gut says drugs. Sell house catering to drug dealers. Pot, ecstasy."

Cav felt his lips twitch. Jones had asked the right questions and was coming to the expected conclusions.

"Last place. The farm? Meth lab. Grow house. Or grow barn. My guess." He took the camera out of the bag. Ran through the pictures. "The Jag doesn't fit."

Jones was quiet for a while. "Same realtor? Rental agent? Property manager?"

Cav shook his head. "Not supposed to be up for sale or rent. That's one of the areas you have to investigate."

"So how do they tie together?"

"The owners have one thing, no two things, in common. All the owners are elderly, and all live in the same retirement community, Forest."

Jones pressed his lips together.

Cav waited for Jones to put it together.

"Lori," he said. His sister was a physical therapist who worked for herself and had many elderly clients at Forest. And she was dating his boss.

Cav nodded. "Three things in common. But my source is anonymous. And, before you ask, all the owners are believed to be mentally keen. Their homes are vacant and are being watched by neighbors or property management companies. At least the Estates place has a property manager, name of which I don't have. Don't know about the farm."

"Now you know what I know." Cav handed over a slip of paper with the addresses. "I want you to work the case; find the common denominator without tripping any wires. I agree with you. Two properties look like drugs, but let's not jump to any conclusions. Especially since the third, the blue house, appears to be normal. And we shouldn't jump to conclusions based on our guts."

But he was following his gut. So was Lori. She knew something was out of whack. But she probably wasn't thinking drugs. More like attorney or property manager defrauding a client. Which this might be.

"Could any have been sold?" Jones asked. "I mean, these are old people. They forget, right? Or maybe, left it up to an attorney to rent?"

"Don't suggest that to my source. She says these elders are each 'sharp as a tack'. Anyhow, you'll find out. Check with the property appraiser for ownership, go online and review rental sites, sales, recent sales. Google, Zillow, B2B, Airbnb—you know the sites. I'll assign Willis to work with you."

"Why not go to the property management company?" Jones asked and then answered his own question. "Because, if something nefarious is going on, they may be in collusion and we would be giving them a heads-up."

"Nefarious? Collusion? You put those two words in the same sentence as heads-up?"

"They're good words. Fit the situation. Couldn't think of one for heads-up."

Cav started the engine. "Go back to the Estates house. Take the undercover truck. Maybe stick a landscaping sign on it. I want photos of every vehicle you see go in or out. Get me twenty-four-hour coverage."

"Will do, Boss."

Back at his office, Cav called the District Attorney, happy to find him working. Cav advised him on a case they'd closed overnight. He met with his second, Chavez, to determine how they were going to catch the dirtbag who was beating homeless men. Then he poured himself a cup of coffee. Cop coffee. He smiled, thinking of Lori's coffee that morning. He took his full mug to his office and made a start on his in-box which sometimes appeared to be bottomless. If he spent an hour first thing every morning on his in-basket, he could keep it under control. It was a necessary drudgery, though he'd rather be in the field. Even on rainy days. He could watch people huddled over, hurrying to their destinations in a city which somehow seemed quieter. He didn't have to worry about rain today. The sun was bright. The air crisp. His morning in the field had been good.

He sorted through reports, wants, and wanted, signed three forms, and dropped everything into his outbox. Done, he leaned back in his chair and swiveled to look out the window at the street. He had been uncomfortable with the window behind him, and it had distracted him when he faced it, therefore, he'd placed his desk perpendicular to it. Sometimes it still made him uneasy, but he could swivel and have a good view which helped him think.

He didn't doubt Lori's observations, if she said the owners of the homes were competent, they were. But he'd have to see for himself. Without violating HIPAA. In spite of the caveat he had given Jones, he was sure they'd discovered two illegal drug operations. The questions were what types and were they connected.

The Estates property definitely felt like a drug sales/supply operation. People coming, staying a few minutes, leaving. But he'd never heard of such an operation in the suburbs. Inner city street dealers, sure. Happened all the time. Sell houses opened and closed randomly, more now it seemed since there had been an influx of drugs in the area. But homes in the suburbs? That was new.

Could be money laundering, he supposed. Money counting,

packaging. He agreed with Jones, not white slavery, the vehicles would stay longer.

He gave it some more thought. Wondered if they should be tailing the vehicles when they left 2185. Decided, no. Photos would be enough for now. Tags and drivers. Run both. When they knew more, BOLOs would find them. By then they might have enough for search and arrest warrants.

The farmhouse was very different. No activity. House boarded up, abandoned. But why the car? High-end, parked. Why not hide it in the barn? Because they were growing product in there? Cooking meth? If so, why no guards? Or were the guards hidden?

The blue house? He'd been watching that house a long time. Since he was a kid. It appealed to something inside him. The woman Jones had spoken with came across as innocent, as just what she said she was. A housewife waiting for her newly built home to become available. How did that fit in with drugs? Did it fit in?

What was the connection between the three properties? First glance pointed at the retirement community. That could make sense. He was pretty sure Jones would come back with just what Lori had told him. No sales or rentals by the owners. And what would that mean? They would check property management firms, too, even if the blue house didn't have one. He didn't have enough information to look at attorneys, or doctors, or hospitals. Should he tell Jones to look into managers at Forest? Employees? No. Jones was good; he'd get there himself. If not, Cav could always suggest it.

Could any of the three properties be rentals? An attorney may have decided to handle the property in the best interest of the client while the client was ill or recuperating. Rent as a source of income to offset the retirement expenses. Could an attorney do that without explicit authorization? Could property managers?

These questions rolled around in his head, but his thoughts drifted to Lori. He'd been surprised how much he didn't want her to dump him. Didn't like the idea. He was comfortable with their relationship. They worked well together. She made him happy, made him laugh.

He stayed at her place three or four nights a week, and she seemed satisfied with the arrangement. He didn't like the idea of splitting up. Why? He'd been dumped before. That was part of life. But he wasn't ready for Lori to walk away. Wouldn't let her. He'd fix whatever the problem was. But first she had to tell him. She had a problem, he was sure, but she wasn't ready to share.

He swung back to his desk. Property managers. How did they work? What did they do? What were their responsibilities? He needed help. So, he'd ask an expert. He picked up his cell and called Kevin, his go-to guy for all things real estate. Kevin, realtor and attorney, would have the answers.

Cav exchanged pleasantries and then asked his question. "What if I say I'm going to go live in a commune in Florida to take care of my aging Granny Iris. And start a charter fishing business. Should I call my attorney and tell him to hire a property manager to take care of my condo, just in case things don't work out and I decide to come back? Is that the way it's done?"

There was a long silence.

"Kevin? You there?"

"Yeah. Massaging my hurt feelings that you didn't call me first."

"I did call you. Just now."

"No. I mean to manage your condo. I think I'll assume you're using another guy you have a longer relationship with and move on to, 'I'm sorry to hear about your grandmother in Florida.'"

"Kevin, I don't have a grandmother in Florida."

Another long silence.

"Kevin?"

"Yeah, I'm still here. You're going to Florida to become a charter fishing captain. Quitting your job?"

Cav rubbed his forehead, pulled his hair at the nape of his neck. "No, Kevin. That was a 'what if'. I'm not planning on leaving town."

He pinched his nose. It was his own fault; he'd thought he was so smart using Jones's made up granny. "Let me rephrase. Let's say some guy I know is going to do that. Would he hire an attorney? A property manager? Both? What are the responsibilities? Limitations? And what is a property manager anyway?"

"Oh. We're not talking about you. Um. Good. Can you even spell boat? That's what I was thinking. Some other guy is going to do that?"

"Yeah. What can the attorney do?'

"Depends. If you told him to manage the property, it would be up to him how to do it. Rent it, maybe."

"No. This guy wants it kept vacant but kept up."

"Okay. In that case the attorney keeps the property safe and maintained. Like you said, the guy would probably hire a property manager for that task. It's one of the things they do."

"What does that involve?"

"Lawn maintenance, pool service, housekeeping, repairs—broken refrigerator, water leak, electrical outage—pest control like rats. That sort of thing. My people walk through the property once a week to make sure there are no problems. Depends on the company. Some attorneys only work with condo associations, others with individual homes. They might supervise a remodel, renovate, upgrade, though an attorney would probably choose to hire specialists for that. I would hire my own contractors, people I've worked with and trust."

"If the attorney hires his own contractor, does the property manager still manage?"

"Depends, again."

"What about renting? Who would do that?"

"Either one, though, again, I'd want to be hands-on with any rental. Background checks, taxes. Stay in compliance with state law and condo association rules."

"Could you rent without my permission?"

"No. And before you ask, yes, that permission has to be in writing, a contract. Specifying time, minimum rent, deposit for clean-up. That sort of thing. I could fax you a copy of the contract if you want."

"What if you rented it anyhow?"

"Wouldn't happen. But if it did, it would be a breach of contract and a criminal offense."

"Okay, you've helped clarify the process for me."

"You're really not going to Florida?"

"No. Kevin. I am not." He pulled his hair. "Don't start that rumor, I haven't got time to deal with all your family members calling me up." Kevin's family was a group of unrelated people. The family core called themselves the Gang of Five. "This is work related."

"So, if you're not going to Florida, what's up?"

He should never have started his questioning with that statement. "Something we're looking at. Might be nothing. Hard to tell. Early stages. I trust you will keep our conversation private."

"Sure. Hey, did you hear? Khalen popped the question."

Khalen. Cop. Detective from up north. Cav had met him when Becca was shot. Khalen was her partner at the time and helped track down her shooter. Becca was part of Kevin's family. Khalen, nearly so.

"Huh. Took him long enough. What did she say?" Khalen and Mary Lee—ML—had become pretty serious.

"Said yes of course. Khalen was the only one who didn't know she would."

Cav hadn't been certain. Oh, he was sure she loved Khalen, but he wasn't sure marriage was something ML did. ML had always seemed single.

"They haven't set the date yet," Kevin added.

Cav had a sudden vision of a bride in white. Only it wasn't Mary Lee. It was Lori. He caught his breath. Where had that come from? First the *l* word. Now a bride. He didn't panic. Instead, a calmness spread through him. It was love. He loved Lori. And he knew what he'd do next. The logical next step.

"Cav? You still there? You hear what I said?"

"Um." He dragged his attention back. Tried to pull out Kevin's words. "She almost popped the question herself?" he said.

"Yeah. Then she decided, if he wasn't brave enough to ask her to marry him, he wouldn't be strong enough for her. Going to be an interesting marriage." Kevin laughed.

"Hey, Cav, you coming to Sunday dinner? We'll turn it into a celebration for ML and Khalen."

Family dinner. Kevin's family. The gang, five people, none of them related by blood. The gang had added Cav to their 'family'. He smiled at the thought. He'd started as the cop they called when they needed help, graduated to a family member. He'd been born into his own large and loud happy family, but he'd been moved in a way he didn't understand when these people had 'adopted' him. He admired them. Each had overcome tremendous odds to become a success. Every Sunday they had dinner as a family, and he had an open invitation. One or another called to remind him of the meal every week. He didn't know how they decided whose turn it was.

"Can I bring a date?" he asked without thinking.

"You got a girl? Hey man, great. Bring her on over so we can meet her."

He nodded his head. Damned right, he had a girl. And sometime over the past few months he'd fallen in love with Lori. Correction, he'd fallen in love with her the first time he'd seen her. He was only now realizing it. He thought about that. It wasn't just the sex. He could get that anywhere. No, that wasn't quite right. He didn't want to get it anywhere. He wanted Lori. He hadn't looked at another woman since he'd met her.

He loved her. Everything about her. Always in motion. Smiling, laughing, talking. He loved having her close. Coming home to her. Having morning coffee with her. He loved the way she made coffee, dammit.

Thinking of her brought calmness. How could that happen? She was energy personified. He loved her energy. Her passion. Passion for her work, her patients, and, yes, for him.

When he slept at his condo and woke alone, he missed her. He wanted to go to bed every night and wake every morning with her beside him.

"I got a girl," he growled. They'd kept their relationship quiet because of her brother and how it might affect Jones at work. Wouldn't Kevin be surprised to find out he already knew Cav's girl. That she was a friend of the gang. A good friend. He smiled at the thought.

His other line was squawking at him.

"Gotta go." Yep. He'd take Lori with him. The gang already treated her like a sister. Lori had earned her place in the family. He thought about her problem, hoping it wasn't him. What was she doing now?

*

Lori was leading her first balance group of the day. She'd been inspired one day while helping a patient who had spent two weeks flat on her back in a hospital bed. Hospital beds wreaked havoc on muscles. And patients graduating from wheelchairs, crutches, or walkers needed to re-learn to stand and walk. Even healthy older folks tended to become unsure of their steps which caused them to sit more, causing loss of mobility, so she always had at least one balance class a day where patients re-learned to walk, bend, stoop, dance. Every day she helped someone. Taught them how to manage their pain, increase their flexibility. Gave them goals and set up exercises to reach those goals. She loved her work. She loved every aspect of patient interaction: observing to determine the problems, establishing plans, evaluating and recording progress. Loved helping people.

She was at her most energetic in the morning, so that's when she worked with clients. She took a late lunch, when her body slowed down, then completed paperwork, billing, and scheduling in the late afternoon and evening. Not as much fun, but necessary. She liked being busy and planned her days that way. And today she was busy.

Busy kept her mind off her problem. No, it didn't, because she had to tell him. Today. She'd tell him today. She stomped her foot. She faced her problems head on. Dealt with them. She wasn't a sissy. So why was she having so much trouble telling him?

Today. She'd do it. Tonight, she would talk to him. She wouldn't put it off any longer. She'd procrastinated too long already. She still wasn't sure why she hadn't told him of the job offer. Why she'd made the decision to accept without discussing it with him. Sure, accepting had been a no brainer. Telling Cav was the hitch. No. Not telling Cav was the hitch. And he knew something was up. She could tell.

She covered her eyes with her palms, swept her fingers across her eyebrows and dragged her hands down to her jawline. Looked in a mirror at herself. She was such a mess. She'd made the decision on her own and now she felt guilty because she hadn't discussed it with him. Why should she? He didn't have a say in how she earned a living. He was just the guy who came over a few nights a week. A guy she slept with. She didn't have to explain herself to him. Tell him every little thing. Check with him.

She really was a mess. There wasn't any reason for her to feel guilty for not discussing it with him. His opinion wasn't that important. Geez. Now she was justifying her own decision to herself.

Her problem was that she did want to talk it over with Cav. Not so much because she wanted his input, but because, damn, she wanted his input. That was the problem. She wanted his input. His input was important. Normally, she would have discussed the opportunity with him. Talked it over with him. But she hadn't. Two weeks now, she hadn't brought the subject up. Because, she realized she wouldn't be discussing it with him as a friend. She'd be talking with the man who could, would, influence her decision.

She didn't know how that could have happened. And she was afraid of what it meant. If his opinion, his input, was important to her, then that meant he was important and that meant she was in trouble. When had their relationship developed to that point? How could her career move depend on a man? How had that happened?

Sure, she liked him. She wouldn't be sleeping with him if she didn't like him. He was a good man. He was a very good man. Honest, fair, considerate. Lori liked him the first time they'd met after she'd taken Becca on as a client after she'd been shot. The bullets had caused considerable damage made worse by the time in a hospital bed and Becca needed extensive physical therapy to get back to par. Becca's family, the Gang, hired Lori because they knew her brother Andy. One or the other of them was always around. Cav hung around, too. And ate. It had taken her a few days to realize this fun guy was her brother's boss, Sheriff Cavanaugh, the perfect cop. Tall, sandy-haired. Quiet. Normal. Not at all what she'd expected for a cop. Which was silly, because her brother was a cop and he was normal. Cav was a good cop. Andy admired him. Becca was a good cop. Said she'd trust Cav to watch her six. And Becca's husband, Gibbs, was an FBI Agent, Lori respected him.

She hadn't meant to get mixed up with her brother's boss, but Cav was interested, and she was attracted. A few dates, then a few hookups, then he started staying over. First, only for a night, then gradually more, and then he'd brought a shaving kit and a few changes of clothes. They both were comfortable with that.

Her cheeks warmed when she thought of the discussion Cav had had with her brother. Cav hadn't mentioned it, but her brother had. "Almost felt sorry for the guy," Andy had said. "He was nervous. Wanted me to know you were seeing each other. But I'd already figured that out. He didn't want me to think he was taking advantage of you." Andy laughed. "As if. I warned him it might be the other way around." Andy put up his hands up and said, "I'll tell you the same thing I told him. I don't want any details. But tell me you like the guy; you're not just messing with him?"

"I like the guy. And don't worry. You don't get details," she'd said.

"He said the same thing, Sis."

She was surprised how long the affair had lasted. Usually her affairs lasted six or seven months. She'd been with Cav over a year. That should have been a warning for her, but she hadn't been paying attention. Too late. And now it felt like a betrayal that she hadn't told Cav about the job offer. How stupid was that? So, she'd just tell him tonight. Get his input tonight. She didn't have to tell him she'd already made the decision to take the job. Let him think she was deciding. Problem solved.

# TUESDAY

She would have told him. She was sure. But Cav hadn't come home. He'd called to let her know he'd be working late, and he'd gone to his own condo. They'd talked briefly on the phone. No opportunity to tell him about the offer. She'd done her paperwork and gone to bed. This morning she woke up alone. And lonely. She missed him. She sighed as she looked over her appointments for the day while sipping cold coffee. Ugh. He always made sure she had hot coffee.

Her phone chimed. Maxine, Mrs. M. The woman was amazing. At seventy-five, she was dynamic and vital. Smart. No memory problems, Cav.

Max didn't say hello. "Lori. I just received a ticket from New York City. A notice lien, they call it. Apparently, I ran a red-light last month. While I was in the hospital. The ticket is over three hundred dollars."

Huh? Good, a new problem. Lori asked for the web address on the ticket and typed it into a search engine. The official NYCServe, eService center. The site was simple to navigate. She clicked on Parking/Camera Violation where she could search by either violation number or plate number and entered the violation number and hit search. A picture of the car, tag number, and the date and time of the violation came up. "Hm. Is that your car? Your tag number do you know?"

"Yes, it is. I have my car registration right here. But my car has been parked in the garage since I fell four months ago. I've never taken it to New York. I only drive to the grocery store and the library."

Lori wondered if the car was in the garage. If unknown people were living in Max's house, it was possible they were driving her car. She could go over to the house and peek in the garage. She considered the ramifications for a moment and decided it would be better to turn the problem over to Cav.

She was glad now she had told him about the properties. Hadn't been sure if she should bother him, but something was going on. She read enough mysteries, watched enough TV, to be suspicious. She'd gone to look at the three properties and then she'd talked it over with Becca, her best friend and confidant. Becca had said, "Tell Cav. NOW." So, she'd told Cav about the properties. Didn't tell him about her job offer.

"Max, let me look at this some more. May I come over. Bring a friend? Someone who can help with the legal options?"

"Oh, could you? That would be so wonderful. I'm worried."

"Okay. See you in a bit." Lori checked through the site again, then walked around the room. She'd tell Cav about the ticket and then tell him about her job offer on the way over to Max's.

He answered just as she was beginning to think she'd have to send a text.

"Hey, honey," he said.

"It's me."

He chuckled. "Yeah. Caller ID kind of tells me that. What's up?"

"Mrs. M has another problem." Lori explained and added, "I made a date for us to go over after lunch and look at her ticket."

"Those red-light cameras are generally accurate. You're sure this woman has it all together, honey? Could she have loaned out the car? Rented or sold the house? Because the people in that place look innocent. The woman says it's temporary lodging provided by their builder while waiting for their occupancy permit."

"You've been out there already?"

"Sure. You were worried."

"Now I'm worried about the ticket."

"Okay. I can look at the ticket. I'll pick you up at home. Give me that code number for the violation, I'll take a look now."

She did, and then hesitated, but realized this was not the time to bring up her job offer.

But he caught the hesitation. "Something else?" he asked.

"No. See you soon."

He found a stale donut in a box in his vehicle (how had he missed that?) and gobbled it down on his way to pick up Lori. But he was still hungry. She was waiting out by his truck. He parked his unmarked sedan and walked around to give her a long kiss. She licked her lips when he leaned back and handed him a sandwich. "Snack."

"I love you," he said. And stopped. He'd said love. Because he said it when she fed him? Was he that crass? Probably. Habit? Maybe. Nodded to himself with a smile. It felt right. Chomped a bite on his way to the passenger side. Bacon, lettuce, and tomato with cheese and an egg on thick rye bread. It should hold him.

She drove ignoring the *l* word. "Hope I'm not wasting your time on this."

"You're not. I saw the ticket. Violation," he responded mid-chew. "And she says she wasn't driving last month?"

"Last month? No way. Her hip wasn't ready yet. No way she drove. And she never drives to the city." She parked in the Forest lot which was mostly empty. He finished the sandwich and they went inside.

Mrs. Mansard studied him when they were introduced and said, "Mr. Cavanaugh. Or should it be Sheriff Cavanaugh?"

He raised an eyebrow.

"Well, you are Lori's friend. And her friend is the Sheriff."

"Yes, Ma'am. But I'm here in a purely personal capacity. As a friend and advisor with some knowledge of the law." He backed that up with an innocent smile.

"Thank you, Sheriff Cavanaugh. I do need help with a legal problem." She gave him the innocent smile right back.

"Cav, Ma'am. Call me Cav." He found Mrs. M—M for Maxine or Mansard—to be one sharp lady. Maybe too sharp. She was observant, astute, and had a sense of humor.

"Call me Max."

"Max, then. Pleasure to meet you, Max." He gave her a real smile.

She motioned to her computer, a laptop on a small side table in front of a window, and pointed to the violation notice sitting beside it. Lori sat and brought up the site, then typed in the violation number and pulled up the screen capture of the tag and the rear of the car. Cav and Max both looked over her shoulder.

"That is your tag?" Cav said. "And your car?"

"It certainly looks like my car. And that is my tag number. The registration is in that folder under the ticket."

He picked up the notice of violation and the folder labeled simply 'new car' and thumbed through it. Bill of sale stapled to the window sticker. She'd paid a few thousand less than sticker price, he noted. Title, registration, insurance. Even maintenance. At the bottom were papers on the old vehicle she'd traded. She kept good records. Supposed she had to, dealing with taxes. He went back to the bill of sale.

"You had the car delivered to your house?" New car? Who did that? Now, sure, but four years ago?

"I called the dealer, told him I wanted to trade my old car for that puddle-jumper—well I didn't call it a puddle-jumper when I talked to him. We settled on numbers that seemed fair to both of us and he delivered it and picked up my trade-in."

Cav had never heard of anyone doing that. Didn't know you could do it. Used cars, sure.

"I saw some vehicles in the parking lot. You think someone took it from there? Are any other residents having problems?"

"My car isn't here. It's still at home. I haven't moved it. I haven't had it out of the garage since I fell, four months ago." She looked at the screen and grimaced. "I haven't," she repeated emphasizing the I.

"Is it possible somebody borrowed it?"

She shook her head. "No. No one could have borrowed it. Could it be some kind of mistake? A tag that looks like mine?"

"The tag's authentic." He had run it. And found numerous hits for illegal parking within the past few months.

"Could someone have stolen the tag and put it on a car that looks like mine?" she asked and then immediately answered her own question. "Why go to all the trouble to steal a tag when you can steal the car?"

"Have you checked to see if the car is still in your garage?"

"No. I was going to ask Lori to do that."

He frowned. "I'll go with her." The car hadn't been there this morning. If the car was in the garage now, someone could have borrowed it on that Friday to run the light in the City, and then returned it to the garage. Borrowed it multiple times. Which they must have done, for the parking tickets to pile up.

"We'll check for damage, too."

"You think it might have been in a wreck?"

"Not one that was reported. Do you need to notify anyone that Lori will be going inside the house? Do you have it rented? Or maybe up for sale?" he asked innocently.

"Neither. It's empty. My neighbor is looking after it."

"Why don't you give me his number and I'll call and let him know someone will be going inside. And we'll need a key."

She gave him a strange look. Considered his suggestion. "I guess that would be polite. I'll write her name down for you."

He wandered around the room while she went for her address book and was standing in front of a wall covered with five framed matted black and white photographs when she came back with the information and another file folder, this one labeled house.

"Lori says you are renting this apartment. Was it furnished or did you move all your things here?"

"Oh, mercy no. This unit came furnished, that's one of the reasons I took it. One of the staff went to my house to get my clothes and those pictures you are studying, and some knickknacks to make this feel more like home." She pointed to a table with crystal animals. "All my furniture is still in my house. I haven't fully decided to move. Why?"

"These photos are really nice."

"Those are my husband's; he was an amateur photographer."

"This one has a different signature."

Lori walked over to look at it more closely.

Max smiled. "I know. That one was a housewarming gift when we moved into the little blue house. It's by a famous nature photographer. Well, at least he was famous twenty/thirty years ago when we bought the house. Byron, my husband, his photography group gave the print to us. It was so sweet and a little embarrassing because we had already bought that print for ourselves. Had it hanging in the den. No one noticed we had two. Always gave us a giggle."

She didn't know the value of this print? And had it hanging on a wall with amateur snapshots. Was that a sign of dementia?

Max motioned them to the two blue floral love seats bracketing the coffee table. A dark blue recliner was set at an angle with its own side table, an open book lay face down on top of it. She poured coffee and watched closely as he thumbed through the file and copied down the name and number of her attorney and lawn service.

"You have a lawn service?"

"Yes." She put her coffee down on the table, leaned forward. "Maybe you two should tell me what's going on."

"What do you mean?" he asked innocent and puzzled.

"You didn't need to see the original ticket; it's posted online. Lori found it. You probably did too. You're a cop. So that red-light ticket probably meant more to you than to either of us. I would expect that you ran the tag. And found something."

He didn't respond right away, trying to decide how much to tell her. As little as possible. Lori didn't even know it all. Actually, he didn't know anything, it was all still suspicion.

"You did," she said. "I can see it in your eyes." She waited for acknowledgement. Studied him. "There's more, isn't there? Lori didn't bring you here because my car ran a red light in the city. There's another reason you're here, and it only peripherally has something to do with my car." She tapped her finger decisively on the table.

He was fascinated watching her work it out.

"You don't think my car is in my garage, do you?"

When he didn't respond, she continued. "The lawn service. You think something is weird with the lawn service, don't you? But how would the lawn man get to my car? Why did you write down my attorney's name? And what is it about that Everglades print has you so nervous?" She pinned him with sharp eyes.

He looked at Lori who smirked an *I told you so* smile. Not senile.

He couldn't believe the old lady had caught his unease over the photo.

"Who are you?" he asked. He should have run her as well as her vehicle, but he'd assumed she was just an old lady who might be confused or senile. He'd totally underestimated her. His mistake. He should have guessed when he saw her size him up when they'd arrived. It wasn't overt, but she'd made an assessment.

He decided to come clean, at least about the photograph.

"The photo is a Clyde Butcher, as you know. That size, framed and matted as it is, is worth right around twenty-five hundred dollars."

Max almost fumbled the coffee she had just picked up. She took a breath and placed it gently on the table.

He smiled at her reaction. "I wondered if you knew."

"And you wondered if I was senile. It was my hip which deteriorated, not my brain. I never thought to price the print, no reason to. We took a vacation in Florida. Byron said the photo was an excellent example of black and white photography. We bought if for about fifty dollars, and I guess I imagined it might have increased in value, but not that much. It's the story, the memories. It makes me happy to see it sitting in the middle of Bryon's photos."

"Butcher's work is very popular and still in great demand. Check his web site."

"And I have two prints," she said and frowned. "Maybe I have two." She took a sip of coffee while she worked through it. "Do you think someone pinched the other?"

He didn't answer. "Could someone have borrowed your car? The lawn service guy?"

"No. I don't see how the lawn guy could get into the garage. He has no reason to go inside."

"Where do you keep your lawn tools? Mower?"

"He has his own equipment."

"Someone else. A relative maybe? A great nephew? Second cousin? Anyone like that? Maybe a contractor who builds houses?"

"No relatives. I have outlived them all. Don't know any contractors."

"A friend? Your neighbor?"

She thought. "No friends who still drive. As for neighbors, Mrs. Weldon's on the left side, she has keys to the house. Not the car. She knows I'm gone and is keeping an eye on the house. The neighbors to the right are new. Same across the street. We say hi."

"Car keys in the house? On a hook maybe? Sitting in a tray?"

She rubbed her eye. "No. They're in my purse."

"A second set?"

"Okay. In a drawer in my kitchen. But Mrs. Weldon doesn't drive."

"But she may have a friend, a younger relative?"

"Well, yes. She has, um, nephews. Three, I think."

"What about people here. New friends. They know you have a home? A car?"

"Well, it's not a secret. Some of us do have homes. But I can assure you no one here is taking my car to New York City."

"Do any have their own vehicles?"

She frowned at him, thinking. "Well, one friend. He keeps his pick-up in the parking lot."

"What's his name?"

"Dennis Kingstone."

"Anyone here who might have a vehicle at their house?"

"Maybe. I think. Vivian does, Mrs. Tubalt. Vivian Tubalt. You think someone may be borrowing her car too? Or Dennis's from the lot?"

He shrugged. "What about management here? Staff? They know your circumstances. They have access to keys?"

She frowned. "You think it may be someone here?" She fidgeted.

That thought obviously made her uncomfortable.

"Don't really think so. Just covering all the bases." Though it would make everything easier if it were someone working here. "What about property managers? Could your friends have the same company?"

She shook her head. "I don't know."

There was no way to soften the next question. "Attorney? He have a key?"

"Wow. Logical suspects. First me. My family, my friends, then the lawn guy, staff here, property manager, my attorney. You have a bigger problem than my car, don't you?"

The woman was scary smart. He made a judgement call. "You can't repeat what I am about to tell you. It can't leave this room. It's part of an ongoing investigation."

Ongoing because Jones had reached him as he left the office. He'd found no records of any of the properties being up for sale or rent. Cav hadn't had time to contact Kevin again, ask him to check. As a professional realtor, Kevin would have access to more files or lists than Jones could find online.

"You too," he said to Lori. Both women nodded.

"I want to be deputized," Max said.

That stopped him. "What?"

"I see that on TV all the time. I want to be deputized. You don't have to pay me," she said quickly. "I just want to be able to say I was a deputy, maybe sometime at a later date, when this is all over. I can be, like, a volunteer deputy. Or a consultant."

He laughed. He couldn't help it.

"I can keep a secret," she added, arguing, entreating. "I worked for the IRS and then as a tax practitioner for close to thirty years. I defended clients in tax court. My husband, Bryon, was a criminal attorney."

Cav felt his eyebrows raise in surprise. At least that helped explain how she'd caught him.

Lori laughed out loud. "Told you Cav. Told you."

"You didn't tell me she was the IRS."

"Only for fifteen years," Max said. "Then I became an Enrolled Agent, that's someone who can argue for clients in tax court opposite the IRS. Tell me about my car," she demanded bringing him back to the reason for the visit.

He hedged. "I haven't even told Lori yet."

"Tell us together. After you deputize me." She waited.

He pulled at his hair and caved. Not for the first time he

wondered about his name. They both stood. "Hold up your right hand."

She did.

"Do you solemnly swear to carry out your duties as a volunteer deputy in the City of Bear and keep secret any information you might learn?"

"I do."

"Okay. You are now an official deputy."

"Where's my badge?"

"Dollar Tree Store."

She laughed. "I have to buy it myself?"

"You're enjoying this, aren't you?"

"Oh, yes. It's the most fun I've had in years."

He gave up. "Okay. Okay. I'll buy the badge. I ran your tags and they came back with multiple parking tickets. Five different days and places, once in front of city hall. We're looking for video footage.

"We also ran the car through ALPR, Automatic License Plate Recognition. That's—"

Max interrupted. "I know what that is."

"I don't," Lori said.

"Cameras, license plate readers, are placed all around town, on bridges, tunnels, toll plazas, automatically snapping photos of license plates. Everywhere. It was first used by tow companies to locate vehicles to repossess. Some companies even hire people to drive around taking pictures. The technology, well, simply put, it takes the image and translates it into the plate number. I'd have to send you to the web for the technical explanation."

Lori shook her head. "Wouldn't understand it."

"Anyhow, we have access and also good rapport with the tow companies, and we can map out where the vehicle has been over the past few weeks. We're checking the addresses now. ACLU is making noises that ALPR is an invasion of privacy, but it's a really good tool for law enforcement."

He stopped and drank some coffee, deciding how much to share.

"So, someone is using my car on a regular basis and you think it's my lawn service guy, Mike," Max said.

Cav nodded. "Or someone working for him. Maybe he's taking it out for a spin whenever he does the lawn. Is he on a schedule do you know?"

"Have no clue. Just once a week, or as needed, random days and times. What are you going to do?"

Cav shrugged. "I've assigned a detail to watch your house."

"Part time or full time?" she asked and sipping her coffee.

Cav hedged. "Part time for now."

"Want me to ask my neighbor about it?"

"No. Could be her. That might tip her off. And we, um, we want to catch her with the car."

Max considered him. She looked at Lori who immediately hid behind her own coffee cup.

"I could go look myself; after all, it is my house. And I need underwear."

Lori stiffened. Cav immediately said, "No."

Max gave him another long look. Leaned forward to set her cup on the table. "You don't assign a detail to watch a house because someone may borrow a car. My puddle-jumper? Someone took it out for a spin because it's such an exciting car? A Corvette, maybe, or a Maserati. Not my car," she said with both disbelief and derision. "I want to know what you're not telling me."

He gave it up. Part of it. "We have reason to believe, based on reliable information, that some people may be taking advantage of residents of this retirement community. Our investigation is just beginning. We need to be careful here. If you do anything now, speak to the wrong person, you might blow our investigation, scare off the perpetrators. Your car is part of a criminal operation."

She studied him. It somehow made him nervous.

"Humph. You're still not telling me what's going on."

"I won't. I can't."

She glanced at Lori who was leaning forward watching Cav intently. Cav saw it. Pulled his hair. The old lady was getting her signals from Lori's body language. He waited. Lori seemed satisfied and relaxed back. Max did also. She nodded. "All right. Do it your way. Don't tell me. Keep your newest deputy in the dark"

Cav breathed. Hadn't realized he'd been holding his breath.

She added a warning. "For a little while. Not for too long though. I like answers to puzzles. How long do you think it will be before you can tell me something?"

"Give me a week." If he needed more time, and he thought he would, he'd be in better shape to negotiate when he had more facts. He wasn't sure the three homes should be lumped together. His gut was telling him her house was different from the other two properties. But the car made him uneasy. Maybe he should send out a meter maid and boot it next time they spotted it. But he had a feeling more was going on with the car too.

She pursed her lips. "Three days."

So they were going to negotiate. He considered her a moment. "Okay. Three days. And I wonder, if as a formally authorized volunteer deputy, you could take on the duty of listening to the folks around here. See if anyone else with a vacant home or condo has noticed anything strange. Don't ask questions, just listen. If you hear anything, give me names, and I'll take it from there."

"Planning on doing that anyway. Don't you want to know if there is a common lawn service involved? Mike? Or property manager or attorney?"

Cav shook his head; she'd have made a good investigator. "No. I'm afraid you can't do that without giving yourself away."

"IRS," she reminded him.

Maybe she could pull it off. She was going to work on it anyway. "Okay. Good. You could perhaps say something like—"

She cut him off. "I know what to say. Trust me."

He reached in his pocket and pulled out a card, wrote on the back of it. "Here's my contact information. My personal cell number is on the back. Call me if you hear anything."

"Thank you. Now sit and visit a minute, can you? Tell me more about my print."

Cav told her what he knew, repeated that she should look at the website, which she did as they watched. They spent a few more minutes with her and left.

"You didn't tell her the whole story," Lori said when they were back in his vehicle.

"No. I didn't."

"You didn't tell her I was your source."

"She doesn't need to know. Though that old lady is so wily, I wouldn't be sure she doesn't. She's seventy, right?"

"No. Seventy-five. I think the seventies are the new young age for old age. Seventies is young and nineties is old. But old doesn't mean senile. There are a lot of people in that community who are both sharp and spry well into their nineties. How do you know the car is not in the garage?"

"The garage door was open this morning when we stopped by. No puddle-jumper. Why does she call her car a puddle-jumper? What is that anyhow?"

Lori went along with his change of subject. "A puddle-jumper is a small plane that flies short distances with only a few people. Think the Alaskan remote area mail plane or passenger transport. This would be the vehicle version."

"Guess I knew that."

"Tell me how you know about a Florida photographer."

"Gibbs. He brought one of Butcher's prints back when they

40

went to Naples for May's baby's christening. He showed us the print at our last poker game. His was a lot smaller. Becca didn't mention it to you?"

Lori frowned. "I guess she did. I wasn't really paying attention. Until tonight, I didn't realize black and white photography was a *thing*. Though Becca did say Ryan was enchanted with a print and she had encouraged him to buy it. She was smug she'd found the right button to push to make him spend money on something he really wanted. She didn't say anything about the print or the cost. I'm surprised Ryan did."

"He didn't. I saw it and looked the photographer up on the web."

"You just hate anyone knowing more than you do."

He glanced at her with a smile. "What about the other two, Mrs. Tubalt and Mr. Kingstone? Are they as sharp as Max?"

"Yes. Why? What are you thinking?"

"Nothing yet. Just collecting information."

They settled into silence for the rest of the ride as he moved pieces of the puzzle around in his head. Like Max, he liked puzzles. He gave her a sideways glance and came to a decision. She was still holding something back. He wasn't going to drop hints to feel her out.

He dropped her off and headed back to the office. He wasn't going to tell her he loved her. He was going to buy a ring and propose. Tomorrow. He would take his chances. Like a man.

But first, he would have to ask Jones for permission.

Jones was waiting with a fat file folder in his hand, excitement fairly sparking off of him. Cav didn't let his smile reach his eyes as he poured a cup of coffee. "Go on in." He motioned to his office and walked over to Sue who handed him his messages and the overnight reports. Today her short gray hair had a pink streak. He shuffled through the messages stopping about halfway, raised an eyebrow. Sue was watching him.

She nodded. "The D. A.?" She pointed to the slip. "He's in court until noon time and will come by after. And Chavez, no message slip, but he has something, and he'll be in around ten."

"Thanks, Sue." Cav walked into his office, sat behind his desk, leaned back, and put his feet up. "What do you have?" he asked Jones.

"Well, on the properties, nothing. No sales or rentals for any of the three houses online and Kevin didn't come up with anything either."

Cav smiled inside. Another gold star for Jones. Contacting Kevin for information.

"There's no way to ask the property management companies without setting off warning bells. Kevin did put out some feelers." Jones held up a hand. "Nothing out of the ordinary. He frequently puts out feelers for a particular type of property. This time he requested a farmhouse with a few acres, out near your farm. And a two or three bedroom downtown, for rent or rent to own. He says realtors do that sort of thing all the time. Too early to hear anything back on either of those. He didn't move on the Estates house because there's a lot of property available in that area and it would look suspicious if he had to ask."

"Neither of us could find any connection between the properties except the obvious. The owners live in Forest. They come from different walks of life. Dennis Kingstone, the farm owner, moved into Forest voluntarily when he became ill. That's what a neighbor says. The two women, Mrs. Tubalt of the Estates house, and Mrs. Mansard of the blue house, were both fall victims. They went to different hospitals, had different doctors, moved into Forest at different times."

"Yeah, I was afraid of that. Nothing to do but interview them. Don't want to do that. One of them might be our man. Or woman." Cav grimaced. "I think I might have an idea, though." He changed the subject. "Willis out at the Estates house?"

42

"Yeah. With Harper. Traffic in and out slowed down after you left. Got photos." He held up the file and Cav detected a note of tension. He stood and walked to the credenza and cleared the surface, pushing everything into a pile in a back corner, then Jones laid out the photos. Each photo had a time stamp and GPS printed across the bottom.

"Eight cars. We saw two orders of pizza go in last night. Seemed strange. Pictures are here." He pointed. "One was a real delivery. The other, I think, another buy." Jones continued laying down photos. "Of the eight vehicles, seven out of state," He pointed to the tags. "Not surprising as we're central to New Jersey, Pennsylvania, New York, Maryland, and D.C. One from Delaware—Wilmington." He paused.

"First car, side view, driver's side turning into the driveway. Rear view with tag." He slapped them down. "Front of the vehicle exiting the drive, view of the driver. Last photo, right side of the car and passenger."

He laid out additional papers and photocopies in a row. "Each vehicle. Registration. Wants and warrants on the vehicle. Owner. Owner's license, and rap sheet. Drivers match the pictures on their licenses."

Cav nodded.

Jones continued. "Vehicle two." He put these down in a new column. "Note the mailbox in the background of each shot. Matches the GPS stamp."

"How did you get these?" Cav asked. "Wasn't anyone suspicious?"

"House across the street. I asked the property owner if we could use his driveway. Found out he'd already called in three complaints about cars coming and going across the street. Said the woman who owned the house had moved out and the property was supposed to be empty. Then traffic started going in and out about three weeks ago. The local precinct sent out a car, but nothing happened.

Anyhow, this guy let us park on his property with an excellent view across the street. We just snapped pictures, kept a written timeline."

He held up a leftover cookie. "The wife fed us cookies and sandwiches. Wanted a tour of the van's interior. They'd seen that kind of vehicle on the TV cops shows. Hope that was okay," he said, showing some nervousness.

"Good public relations," Cav said and hid his smile. The kid was good, sharp. Didn't miss much. Still a little green around the edges, but that was wearing off. Cav had no doubt the kid would be sitting in his chair in a few years, just hoped he'd be ready to retire before that happened. But Cav thought Jones had another problem.

Jones said, "We could stop any one of the vehicles. They all have violations. This last one, here? Big black SUV. Missed the turn and had to come back. We got a really good shot of both the driver and the passenger." Jones pulled his hair.

Hunh?

"I'm sorry, Sir, but I screwed up on this."

Yep, another problem, Jones never called him Sir. Jones handed the photos to Cav.

He took them, wondering why the kid thought he had screwed up.

Looked at the blowup.

"Shit. Brouska. What's he doing here?" Cav couldn't keep the frustration out of his voice. They called him Brouska because no one could pronounce his real name, Brouskovetski. "I was hoping the rumors of his death were true." Wiped his hand down the back of his head and tugged on the hair at his neck. Was it getting long? "Damn."

The second photo stopped him short. "Eggert. Double damn. Eggert's with him? Both of them? Together?" He rubbed his forehead.

"I'm sorry, Sir. I should have followed him."

"You recognized him when you took this photo? With that long lens?"

"No Sir. Not until it was enlarged. I screwed up, Sir."

"Jones. Stop calling me Sir. Did you tail any of the other vehicles?"

"Ah, no, Sir. But I shoulda tailed this one."

"How could you have known that at the time?"

"Could have enlarged the digital in the camera viewfinder, Sir."

"Hmm. Hadn't thought of that." Cav pulled his hair. "Stop calling me Sir. I'm not sure that was an oversight. Did you enlarge any of the others?"

"No Sir, um Boss. Figured they were all low-grade dirt bags. That's what we were finding when we ran the tags."

"What about the tags on this vehicle? You run them? And if you didn't, you'd better call me Sir."

"Rental."

"Follow up on that?"

"Got name and address and credit card. But the card comes back to an old guy. Probably stolen and not yet reported. Checking that."

"Everything you did sounds reasonable to me under the circumstances. I am satisfied with your actions. Moving on. We'll have to notify the Fibbies. They'll want to know. Eggert killed two of theirs."

Cav's cell pinged, hiccupped, he looked at the screen. "Kevin. I asked him to put his drone up and take pictures. Had to listen to a long-involved description of his new drones and which one might work best for my purposes. Seems one of them can talk." Cav shook his head. "Told him to decide but get me the license on the Jaguar parked at the farmhouse. And keep the drones silent. Told him to fly over the Estates property too."

He looked at his cell again. Kevin had sent photos accompanied by a text, naming the drone Kevin used and why. It said he had no luck with the Jag, but there were three vehicles visible at the Estates house which also had a three-car garage. Doors all shut.

Cav ran through the pictures of the Estates quickly then moved on to those of the farmhouse, about a dozen. He went through those slowly and stopped at the first one of the Jag, enlarged it. But no matter how he played with it, he couldn't see the tag. Enlarged the Jag windshield but couldn't make out the decal or see the VIN, vehicle identification number. Searched the next Jag photo. Felt Jones go still beside him, looked over.

"Stop. Back up one."

He swiped backward. Saw what Jones had seen. His eyes went back to Jones. "Shii-it." Wiped his hand over his head, pulled his hair. "Not meth." He moved through the remaining photos quickly. Handed his cell to Jones. "Get these printed and enlarged. Pay special attention to those boxes behind the barn and the Jag decal."

Jones hurried off. Cav waited and examined the men in the black SUV. "You son of a bitch. We've got you now." Maybe.

Jones came back a few minutes later with the blow-ups. Two sets. They both sat and looked through them.

"That's three pill-press boxes." Cav laid the photo on his desk frowning. In addition to the press boxes, there were blocks of cement and lumber, which were commonly used to stabilize the pill-presses. The dusting of white powder around the door and the hayloft meant oxy, fentanyl, flour. "They're making pills, opioids. How long have they been doing it? Since Kingstone moved out? Explains the surge in sales and deaths around here."

He groaned. "We can't sit on this. Going to have to call in help. We certainly don't have the training to take down a fentanyl lab. Or to clean it. Need a special team for that. Damn." He leaned forward in his chair, pulled his hair. "We would have had to call them in anyhow, with Eggert involved." Cav picked up the photos of the black SUV. "Brouska and Eggert. Together. Thought Eggert was out of the country." Shook his head. Thinking. Made a decision.

"All right. We call in the FBI. We keep control."

Jones let out a snort.

"Gibbs. I'll call Gibbs. Fuck going through channels. We go direct to Gibbs. Yes. Gibbs can do it. Gibbs will work with us. And drugs going across state lines means we need to call in DEA. Agent in Charge, though, Dawson. Not his new guy. Doesn't work with us so we leave him out of the loop. We take down the dealers first. Has to be a way to play it so the dealers don't know how we found them. I don't want them to track us back to Forest."

He glanced thoughtfully over to Jones. "You said all those vehicles had wants. Maybe we wait for one to come out of there and run the stop sign at the end of the street. Have a squad car handy to stop him. Wanted felon, we search him, search the car. Make it look like the violation led us to the sell house and that led us to the farm. We can get these dealers, the local ones. But out of state and the pill makers, for that we need the Fibbies. And Brouska and Eggert add a whole level of complexity."

He did that thing with his hair again. Dammit he'd have a bald spot by the end of the day.

"Call Kevin, see if he has anything new on the real estate. I'll call Ryan."

They both got busy with their cells. Cav scrolled through his contacts, selected Gibbs. It rang three times before it was answered.

"Gibbs."

"Hey, Ryan. I need a favor." Wasn't going to make the same mistake he had with Kevin giving him a scenario.

"This better not be work related, because I am on vacation."

"Are you in Bear?"

"Damn, Cav. Yes, I am in Bear. You absolutely cannot have a work problem."

"Sure I can. You're on vacation in Bear. You should expect to be dragged into an operation if you're on vacation. That's why you come to Bear for a vacation, right? Because your day to day work is boring. Way I hear it, the vacation doesn't even have to be in Bear. I heard through the grapevine that your last two rest and relaxation trips to Naples resulted in major crimes solved. That first vacation in Naples you were involved with an art theft and a drug dealer. The second visit, that was just last month, right? Wasn't that when you helped the locals with wine forgeries and a murder?"

"I do not know what you are talking about. Locals did all that. I was on vacation. Rest and Relaxation. R&R." Not the way Cav had heard it. Locals got the credit, but they were quick to tell him that Gibbs made it happen.

Just because Cav needed a favor was no reason not to razz Gibbs. "Maybe, instead of calling it R&R, you should call it A&A, Arrest and Apprehend, or C&R, Catch and Release because you turn the crooks over to the locals, or you could call it C&L, Catch and Lock-up. Next vacation you could try a CFZ, Crime Free Zone." Cav was on a roll.

"This is the way you ask for a favor, Cav?"

"Well, yeah. You at the gatehouse?" Kevin's gatehouse.

"Uh-huh."

"Can I come over?"

"Can I stop you?"

"No. You need to hear what I have. I got a few fires to work on first. But maybe in a couple of hours."

Gibbs sounded resigned. "I'll be here in my crime free zone."

Cav was smiling when he hung up. Didn't get much opportunity to hassle Gibbs. The man was the best cop he knew. Sharp, quiet, observant, and a good interrogator, he had a knack for getting information. Cav was lucky to be able to call on him.

He looked over at Jones who was smiling at the part of Cav's conversation he could hear. "I like that catch and lock up. I have unmarked cars driving past the farm every half hour or so. And Kevin's sending the drone back. I've got something to check, and then I'll go sit on the Estates house. The Mrs. probably has more cookies."

"Be careful. With Brouska and Eggert, don't take any chances," Cav warned following Jones out. He went over to sit with Chavez. "Tell me how you're going to handle this guy beating up our homeless citizens."

Chavez laid out a plan which made Cav smile. "I like it. Heavy on manpower, but workable." They worked on his plan, selecting personnel and locations. The cops would be waiting for the mugger when he went to work Wednesday night.

Cav updated Chavez on the three properties and Eggert and Brouska. Then he said, "I have two questions. The first question. What was Mrs. M's car doing in New York City? Something nefarious maybe." Love that word, he thought and almost became sidetracked at the word love. No time to think about love now. But he smiled.

"The second question is multi part. How do the drug traffickers know which buildings are available and for how long? And related to that, has this drug ring used other residences? Do they make a practice of using empty homes?" Cav felt these were not the first two houses to be used this way. "The drug dealers had to have tried it before. Which means they have abandoned houses. What happened to those homes? Did they clean them up? I doubt it. So what happened when the homeowner, property manager, or attorney stopped by? Was damage or vandalism reported? Did our office receive an official complaint? Was there a burglary or fire? Have someone check our records. I'm thinking we may be able to backtrack them. Find out how they are getting their information."

He paused. "I want the man behind this. Not just Brouska and Eggert. Neither one of them is smart enough to have set this up. They're leg-breakers. So there is at least one more person running this operation. Get together with Jones; he's gone back out to the Estates house."

"Will do, boss."

Cav worried the problem until he reached Kevin's property and the gatehouse, where he plugged in his code, spoke his secret password into the microphone, and winked for the camera. The arm raised and then the gate rolled open.

The security, both digital and physical, was designed by Kevin and his gang of geeks It wasn't extreme or overkill but what was needed to keep everyone safe, because trouble had come looking for the gang on a few occasions and probably would again.

Cav parked and walked into the gatehouse where Gibbs was sitting in the rocker reading a blue binder. He marked his spot, looked up over his glasses and nodded to the coffee pot. "It's fresh. I put it on twenty minutes ago."

Cav wasn't surprised Gibbs had made a good estimate of his arrival time. He poured and, out of habit, checked the fridge. But he wasn't eating yogurt. Gibbs was sort of a health food nut. Cav spotted a bakery box which, upon inspection, held bear claws. He grabbed a paper plate and popped three onto it and came and sat across from the rocker on a small sofa. Took a sip of the coffee which was as good as expected. Gibbs made good coffee, which always surprised Cav, because Ryan drank tea. His wife, Becca, drank coffee. Gibbs made it for her.

Cav handed the files to Gibbs, explaining how it started, not mentioning Lori. "The first file is what we believe is a drug supply house. The second, we thought was a grow house, but it looks like empty pill-press cartons outside." He didn't have to clarify what that meant. "The third looks like an illegal rental and the vehicle, which is supposed to be parked in the garage, is being used by someone not the owner. Not sure that one will fall in your lap."

Gibbs sighed, shook his head. "Eat your bear claw, let me look through these."

"This is your own fault, Ryan," Cav said as he took a bite. "You should know better than to try to take a vacation. It's almost become a challenge for us to keep you occupied." He ate one claw and finished his coffee while Gibbs read through the folders. Went for a second cup and heated water to make Gibbs some tea. When he sat back down, he picked up the binder Gibbs had been reading. Ryan raised an eyebrow, but went back to the folders.

The binder contained news articles and law enforcement interaction with fentanyl. One article from the *Wall Street Journal* stated law enforcement must 'treat drug seizures like an active shooter incident—slow down and evaluate the scene before entering—ensuring they have elbow-length gloves, protective masks and safety glasses.' Pill-presses were included.

Huh. Looked like Gibbs was studying up on fentanyl. This binder would help Cav's case. He examined the room, noting some changes to the open floor plan. The dining room table and chairs for twelve in the center, surrounded by the four computer workstations along the exterior wall were the same. No boring room dividers like an office separated the workplaces. Each was a separate grouping of comfortable chairs, sofas. The monitors which hung on the walls were large and state of the art. At the end of the room a counter separated the work and dining area from a modern functional kitchen. Beyond that were bedrooms and baths.

This was the room where the gang gathered to work and play, and—he didn't want to think about it—hack into official computer systems. He'd used their expertise on a few occasions. Gibbs had also. They tried to keep it legal. But sometimes one of the gang went off base.

The rocker Gibbs was sitting in was new. One of the computer workstations had been replaced by a bookcase and desk. A tablet and file folders sat on top. Probably Ryan's. A wooden roll chair was by the desk instead of the beanbag chair Kevin used. Maybe Kevin had grown up. No. Not Kevin.

Ryan read through each folder and piece of paper, then he went back through a second time. When he finished, he sighed and stabbed Cav with a glare. "You are taking lessons from the gang on how to spoil my vacations." He sighed. "You know what's happening, where it's happening, and who is making it happen. What do you need from me or the FBI?"

"I need help, but I want to keep some control. A fentanyl factory requires special units, a trained crew with safety gear. Might need them at the Estates house too. I don't have those people. DEA does, but DEA's new guy in charge? He doesn't play well with the locals and I want to do this my way. You can get me to the big boss."

He took another bite.

"I don't want to lose these creeps and I need manpower to surveil them, take them down. Right now, we're doing random drive-bys on the farmhouse, but we need to watch full time. And those drug gang lowlifes hijacking homes is an abuse that fries my butt. And I want Brouska and Eggert. For now, I'm going to get RV SPY. Stick some people in it to watch the farm. I was thinking two of my people—Officer Wilson and Sergeant Chavez—but I have them busy on another stakeout. And since the RV is Kevin's, he'll probably want to be there. A young couple would work."

"Jones?"

"Could be, though he might have been spotted with my truck when we first watched the farmhouse," Cav said, "and he'd be better as a liaison with you folks."

"There's always Becca," Ryan said and then narrowed his eyes. Cav smiled innocently. Was proud of how he'd set Gibbs up to walk right into that. Cav had hoped Gibbs would suggest his wife. Ex-cop Becca Travis Gibbs. He pushed the idea.

"She's worked in the RV before and sometimes consults with you and the FBI. She's here with you, isn't she? At the gatehouse."

Gibbs was shaking his head with a smile. "Yeah, and bored, since I seem to be working." He sighed again. "Put her with Kevin in the RV. Get Kevin down here. I'll call Becca," Ryan said.

Cav pulled out his cell and dialed. "Kevin, I need to borrow RV SPY for a few days, maybe a week."

"You're driving to Florida. Not flying."

"What?" Cav pulled at his hair. Annoyed with himself. "No. I'm not going to Florida."

"Then why do you need RV SPY?"

"Got a thing going with Gibbs here and we need it for a command center. Can you let us have it?"

"Oh, great. I was looking for something to do this week. When do you want us?"

"Now. Becca's going with you. Gibbs is getting her. And Kevin, I know I don't have to tell you, but no one else can know what we're doing."

"Lips are sealed. I'll pack some overnight things."

Cav hung up and said, "There's more I want, Ryan."

"Okay. Tell me."

"I don't want to surveil these men for months. People are dying. I don't want that stuff on the street. I want them busted tomorrow. The next day, latest."

"You have a plan?"

"Take down the supply house in the Estates. Got a couple of ways we could do it without scaring anyone off. Then we can sit on the barn; they're not killing anyone until the next delivery. We follow them and take the truck when they reach the delivery destination. Get the buyers, backtrack them to the origin, get them too. Or, if we have enough people, hit them all at the same time. Get Brouska or Eggert."

"Okay. We can help with surveillance and the take downs. You looked through my binder, so you know we have seen an increase in sales, centered, we thought, south of here in D.C. But based on what you've found, we can assume the drugs are being made here, originating here."

Cav agreed but cautioned, "You know, it could just be pot at the

Estates house. From what you have in your binder, the cartel is still making big bucks on illegal pot sales. Growing it here in the states and transporting it."

"Yeah. But we know it's fentanyl in the barn. No reason they can't be selling both. Fentanyl is scary stuff and we have three specially trained teams. I'll have a talk with Dawson at DEA." He pulled out his phone and added. "I want Eggert. You can have the drug bust, Brouska. I get Eggert. I'll have Dawson tell his new guy how it is going down. And I'll call our fentanyl specialist, Dylan, let him know what we have. His team can work with Jones, Becca. He has some nice toys."

Cav took the file over to the dining room table and laid out the Estates house photos, much as Jones had. "There was a lot of traffic in and out when we first got there. That slowed in the afternoon, and there have only been a few vehicles in since then. We could take one or two buyers out on traffic violations. Go in there, with an emergency response vehicle or a SWAT truck, take 'em down. Put our guys in and play it for a day or two. Pick off the buyers/dealers one by one. Buying with intent to sell."

"Could work for a few hours. Until someone needs to check in."

"Or we take them all down at the same time. Either way."

Gibbs nodded. "Like that idea." He tapped one photo. "Eggert. We want him. He killed two FBI agents before he fled the country."

"Figured you'd want him. Tracked the vehicle. Tags came back to a rental. No leads on Eggert. We want him too."

Gibbs let it drop. "What about this decal?" He pointed to the blowup of the Jag.

"Kevin sent his drone over for us. He got a slightly better image." Cav pulled out his phone and scrolled to the picture. "I'll send it to the monitor."

They both studied it, but Cav still couldn't make anything out.

"We'll see it in person soon enough," Gibbs said. "Get another bear claw; bring me one too, and let's look at your third house."

Cav's cell was buzzing. He pulled it out, looked, and gave Gibbs a crooked grin. "You're gonna love this. My new undercover operative at the retirement home. Max. She owns the third house. The blue house. She is retired from the IRS, had her own tax practice. Her husband was a criminal lawyer." He pushed a button. "Yes, Deputy, I have you on speaker phone. What do you have for me?"

"I found a few more folks who live here and still own their homes. Homes which are unoccupied."

"You were careful, right? You didn't ask any questions?"

"I didn't ask, Sheriff. Why would I do that? Everyone here knows I'm in a dither about whether I should sell my house or rent, or move back. Everyone here wants to tell me what to do. What they did. How they did it. And, to add good measure, how they got here in the first place. I don't have to ask any questions, just listen. Isn't that why you deputized me?"

Now Cav grinned at Gibbs. "Yes ma'am. That why I deputized you. Tell me the names."

"You're not listening. I have quite a few names."

"Hold on, I need to get my notepad."

"Oh, don't waste your time writing everything down, I can email it to you."

"No, you don't need to do that, just read off the names."

There was a long silence.

"Max? You still there?"

"Young man, I am not going to spell out all these names for you. I put everything into a spreadsheet. Though, I could convert it to a database if you prefer. Which do you want? The Excel spreadsheet or the Access database. Both are searchable, though I think Access might be better for your purposes."

"Just how many people are we talking about?" Cav glanced at Gibbs.

"It keeps changing. I can't believe how many people living here want to tell me what to do." She paused. "Fourteen people."

"Fourteen?" Cav could barely speak. Noticed his hand grabbing at his hair.

"Fourteen. Yes. Aren't you listening? Of that number twelve are residents here. Word got out about my dilemma and two old ladies in another retirement home sought me out with stories and advice."

She laughed. "It's a little like sitting on a park bench and throwing out birdseed. Suddenly you're surrounded by birds and squirrels. You'd be surprised, I'm surprised, by the personal stuff people told me voluntarily. They want me to know about their homes. Who manages their property: neighbors, or relatives, attorneys, or property managers. It's all in the spreadsheet. No addresses, because that would have entailed **asking** questions." She put emphasis on asking. "I'm sure you won't have any trouble finding those. Best source would be an old white pages phone book. I included some doctors and hospitals because I had the data."

Her tone changed. "And I must thank you, because this whole investigation has helped me with my decision. I've decided to stay here. I like it here and I like the people. And I've made a lot of friends. We're a great big extended family. We have trips everywhere, you know, sightseeing, shows. Even transportation to doctor appointments and the grocery store. Though why I need to go to the grocery, I don't know. The meals here are wonderful. But sometimes I just need to shop. Sorry, I got distracted. I will sell my house, just not yet, I am not quite ready."

"Ah." It was all Cav could fit in watching Gibbs laugh silently at him.

She paused. "I also have a column, or field, for current status of the houses. I wish I could say that I used my great fact-finding skills, but these folks keep no secrets."

Cav finally found his voice. "Well, Deputy, you have done an amazing job. Good work."

"I'm not done, yet, Mister Cavanaugh," she said, sounding just like an IRS agent. He shut up, mostly because he didn't know what he was going to say. She waited for him to make an acknowledgement.

"Yes, Ma'am. Please continue," he said as politely and respectfully as possible.

"One lady told me her home had been vandalized. I added the extra column because I thought you'd want to know. There are only four places listed in that column. I didn't feel as if I could ask."

Cav grabbed his hair between his fingers and tugged. This time over his ear. A variation he guessed of pulling at the nape of his neck. His second question answered.

"Another woman says her property manager comes here to Forest once a month and takes her to walk through her home. I like that idea. While I keep mine, I think I'll hire him."

Before Max could get sidetracked again, Cav said, "Deputy, I was just discussing your situation with Agent Ryan Gibbs; he's listening in and is a little in awe at everything you have accomplished."

"Nice to meet you Agent Gibbs. You can call me Max. What kind of agent are you? Because I'm done with the IRS."

"FBI, Ma'am, I wonder if you would like to work for me?"

"Oh, my yes. That would be exciting. Would I have to quit my job with Mr. Cavanaugh? Would I get a badge?"

Both men laughed. "You may work for both of us at the same time, and I'll get you a badge."

"The Sheriff was going to buy a cheap badge at the dollar store. Will you get me one of those wallet things they have on TV?"

"A wallet and badge, Max. Tell us again. You are not actually asking anyone questions? Residents of your community simply tell you these things?"

She sighed deeply. "I told Sheriff Cavanaugh I know how to get information without asking questions. I'm not interrogating these people. If one says they use a property manager, I ask who he is, maybe I should hire him. They expect me to ask. Or if they say, they had to leave their home because they fell or became sick, I sympathize, and they volunteer all the gory details. Like the lady who fell the first day she was home on crutches and lay on the floor until the neighbor came. She couldn't get up and couldn't drag herself to a phone. Now she keeps her cell in her pocket. I ask 'Oh, what hospital? doctor? will you go to him again?' You know, people our age, we're always comparing experiences."

"Sounds reasonable, Ma'am."

"If you want to know more, you should talk to my friend, Mr. Kingstone. Oh, I have to go. The bus is leaving for the mall. Shopping and dinner. I'll send the data. Or do you want it on the cloud?"

"Send it as an Access database. I can convert to Excel if we decide we need a pivot table. And we both thank you for your contribution." Gibbs gave her his email address and ended the call. When his cell pinged, he put the database on the large monitor.

"Wow. Look at that. I might really need to hire that woman. She's got all the important factors along with some peripheral elements. All neatly organized."

The database separated property management into attorney, management company, relatives, neighbors. Also listed doctors and hospitals.

"Many of the doctors are the same, I see three, no four listed. She has dates residents moved into Forest. That could be important." He continued scrolling across the field names and moved down through the records. "Looks like most of the residents transferred directly from the hospital. She has original status of home. And current status—sold or given to children, vacant or rented. We can use that. And vandalized properties. Max is certainly detail oriented. Guess it comes from doing taxes. You said she was IRS? She'd have to be detail oriented. How did you find her?" Ryan asked, but he was still sorting through fields. "Here." He pointed. "Sorted alphabetically by attorney name. Two show up multiple times. Got to expect to see some of the same attorneys, elder law is a specialty area."

He sorted by property management companies, but none appeared more than two times. Then by neighbors and by relatives. "Kevin is here as realtor/property manager for two of the properties. We should talk to him."

Cav grumped, "Even with all this, there's no common factor, but it's a good start. Print it out? I do better with paper. We need addresses. I'll get my men on it." He pulled out his cell.

"How did you find her?" Gibbs asked again.

Cav was pretty sure Ryan already knew the answer, just wanted confirmation, especially since he had the therapist field highlighted and was pointing with his finger. "Lori. Lori is her therapist. She has nine clients at Forest. She told you about the properties."

Cav chose to ignore the statement. "You'll like Max. She has a Clyde Butcher hanging in her living room." Cav was hoping to distract him.

"Does she know her car may be driving around town?"

"She knows something's up, but she doesn't know what. I wasn't ready to tell her when we talked to her." He hoped Ryan hadn't caught the slip. Changed it to the singular. "I didn't really know anything then. Just knew the car was missing."

"Don't think you really have a choice now. You don't know where the vehicle is?"

"Not yet," Cav corrected him. "Jones is investigating." He looked back at the spreadsheet. Database? "Max has a lot of information." He paused. "Vandalized properties. We run the owners' names, find the addresses, check for police reports. We were doing that anyhow, but this makes it easier."

Cav stood and paced. "We need more information." He glanced at Gibbs, who was laughing at him. "What?" he asked, annoyed.

"You are going to have to talk to your Deputy again."

"Yeah. Yeah." He flopped into a chair, put his head back and stared at the ceiling. He'd never looked at it before. White plaster. The new LED lights Kevin was so proud of. Closed his eyes. Could feel Gibbs waiting.

"I know. I know. I have to talk to Max, again. In person. I'm a little afraid of her. She's like my Mom, my seventh-grade teacher, and my police academy theory instructor, all rolled into one. Argh."

He reached for his hair, then stood and paced some more. Went into the kitchen. Grabbed another bear claw. How many would that make? Didn't matter. He tore off a bite. Eating stopped him from pulling his hair. Resigned, he said, "I'll go talk to Max. We need more information. Might have to talk to this Kingstone guy too. But you're coming with me. After all, you just hired her, and you should meet her. Tomorrow." He'd have some protection, and it might be fun to watch Gibbs and Max parry swords.

"She doesn't fit, you know. Her house doesn't fit. Her car. The other two places are drug related." He shook his head. Sat again with his printout while Gibbs ran more sorts on the database. "In spite of all this information, this really doesn't tell us much. Need the addresses." And the car. He hoped Jones was having more success.

# WEDNESDAY

He spent another night at his own place and didn't like it. Missed Lori. And something had been niggling his gut overnight. Something besides Lori. He had forgotten to address his first question; why was the car going through the toll booth?

He went into the office early, called up the City crime stats for the day the car was caught by the cameras and scrolled through the pages; stabbings, shootings, muggings, thefts, fender benders. All this for one day? Well, it was New York City. He narrowed his search to an hour before the violation. Pulled up a map to locate the scenes. The violation would have to be within a couple of miles of the toll booth. That narrowed it down to one page, and... bingo.

Yes! He pumped his fist. He knew it. Knew it. His gut was right again. A check cashing shop was robbed ten minutes before the toll violation.

He called up the report. Two vehicles were seen in the vicinity of the stick-up. One witness saw a white Dodge van. A second person saw a small gray car, didn't know what make or model. Mrs. M's puddle jumper? A small gray car. How freaky was that?

He thought about it for a few minutes. There had been a spate of check-cashing shop robberies. Check cashing stores were easy pickings, lots of cash. So far no one had been hurt. The thefts were close enough to the border that he'd put on special patrols Friday and Saturday mornings when the robberies had occurred.

Using Google maps, he called up each of the armed robberies. Next, he plotted the plate tracker hits for Mrs. M's car on a separate map and matched those spots to the robberies—locations, dates and times. On four occasions, the puddle jumper had been in close proximity to the robberies. And, almost as good, the puddle-jumper was never logged anywhere else at the time of the other robberies. Good.

He leaned back, rubbing his hand over his mouth then down the back of his head, pulling his hair. Now he had them. He printed out the maps. Studied them. Yup. The puddle-jumper had participated.

*

Jones backed his truck onto the vacant lot beside an F350. Red, jacked up so high the driver would need a stepladder to access the driver's seat. He looked at the house under construction on the adjacent lot, a three-story colonial with front deck and bay windows. Couldn't tell if it would be bricked, painted, or sided. He was checking all the houses the contractor, Newton, was building; this was the third.

He heard buzzing saws and hammering. When he walked to the doorway and looked inside, he saw two men cutting wood on a table. Another, with a clipboard, turned to look at him. "Help you?"

"Ah, yeah. Looking for work. Wondering if you're hiring."

The man looked him up and down, saw a young fit guy in T-shirt, jeans, cowboy boots. Smiled. "Right. You don't look like an inspector. You a day laborer?"

"Um, no." Jones looked around the room at the wood framing and studs, miles of electrical cabling and pipes, and took a chance. "Electrician."

The man nodded. "Maybe. I'm the foreman. Boss might want another electrician. Come on back this afternoon; he's at another site right now. You got papers?"

"Ah, résumé. I'm not licensed in this state. Do I need a license here? I have letters of reference from down south."

The men sawing didn't pay them any overt attention, though the guy holding the wood gave him the once over. They weren't worried or concerned about a stranger on site. Friendly, not suspicious.

"Bring those; he'll want to see them. No, you don't need a license. I meant citizen papers. Boss only hires American citizens. You'd start at minimum union wage."

"Oh. No one ever asked me that before. Everywhere else I worked, the builder never cared. Could pay the illegal workers less. Had to pay me union wage. Sure, I'm a citizen."

"You can leave me your name and phone number, save you a trip back."

Jones said he'd come back. "What's the boss's name?"

"Jeffrey Newton, Newton Homes." He gave Jones a business card. "Everything you need is there."

"Ah, thanks."

Jones went back out to the parking lot and walked to the red truck. It had rivets framing the side windows and along the fenders over the wheel wells. Closer inspection showed the paint job was iridescent. He turned and looked back at the house; no one was watching. He walked around to the far side of the truck and leaned over to check the suspension. The vehicle was jacked up so high he didn't have to lean far. Two steps, which looked like aluminum alloy, led to the driver's door. So that's how the owner got in and out. No stepladder. He walked to the rear where a single flip step led to the bed. Noted the stainless-steel dual exhausts. Out of sight of the house he leaned down again. Stuck the GPS tracker to the inside fender of the puddle jumper parked on the far side of the truck, out of sight of the road. Smiling, he stood and brushed off his hands then went back to his own truck which didn't need steps.

He drove down the street and around the corner, parked on the side of the road, opened his laptop, and called up the tracking program. There was his tracker in the lot, stationary. He pulled up history and saw his trip from the station to the construction site delineated.

Oh, yeah. He sent Cavanaugh a text with the GPS file attached and called him as he headed for the Estates house.

Cav answered. Listened. Smiled. Oh, yeah, he needed to promote this guy.

"Good work, Jones," he said. "Run the builder. Any plates you got in the parking lot. Complaints or crime reports on them. That might give us a lead to whoever is behind this. Gibbs is going to email you a spreadsheet. Find addresses for the names. You might try the phone book in my office." Jones had joked about the white pages often enough. "Ask Chavez for help, he's waiting for your request." He paused and saw Gibbs had the property managers sorted. Two different property management companies. "Oh, Jones, run the property managers for Kingstone and Tubalt. Let us know what you find." He hung up.

He hollered for Chavez who had just strolled in.

"Sit. Look." He handed the maps over. At first, Chavez looked at them casually, and then he sat up straight, jumped up. "Shit. You did it. You got 'em."

"Let's not jump to conclusions."

"Jump to conclusions. This is too much to be a coincidence. You got the suckers."

Cav pursed his lips, holding the smile. "Maybe."

"And. You got the car's current location."

"Jones got it. Parked at a construction site."

"I'll put a detail on that car. It will make the surveillance we have on the shops near the New York border easier. We'll know when they're coming."

Cav shook his head. "Don't need to. Jones put a GPS tracker on the car." He snapped his fingers. "I better get written permission from Max."

"You think we can find some video of that car in the vicinity of any of those four robberies. Or near one of the other three crimes? Or near its new home base in that construction lot?"

"Let's try. There's lots of cameras. Banks, shops, red lights. We know what we're lookin' for now. Small gray car. If the tapes caught it, we should be able to get a look at the perps."

Chavez paused at the door. "How'd you do it?"

"I was looking for that particular vehicle because of another situation. The contractor has his clients in the blue house. And the owner of the blue house received a violation for that car, her car, in New York. I wanted to know what it was doing in the city."

"Was it on our wants list? How did we know it was cited? Why were you lookin' at the violation?"

"Well, let me tell you about that, because it ties into the drug houses." He gave Chavez a short-hand version.

"Gonna be a busy week for us. We got the manpower?"

"No. I've asked the Fibbies to help."

"Oh, man. Those guys will walk all over us and grab the credit."

"I got a buddy. Don't care if they get the credit. We need to shut down the pill makers."

Chavez grimaced. "Yeah, it just burns. To do all that work—"

"We haven't really done all that work, Chavez. If the Feds play nice with us on the drug bust, we may let them play with the check cashing crooks."

"Okay. Okay. I'll get working with those tapes," he said and they both headed out, Chavez to look for video proof and Cav to pick up Gibbs.

"Jones found Max's car," he told Gibbs. "On one of the contractor's job sites. Put a tracker on it. So, I will have to tell her." They both thought about that for a while.

"It would help if we could talk with either Tubalt or Kingstone," Cav said.

"Agreed. I'll do a background check on both of them."

"Due diligence. Add Max and her deceased attorney husband, Byron."

Gibbs just raised an eyebrow at him, nodded.

Cav stopped his hand from pulling his hair by rubbing his scalp while thinking of what he still had to do. Solve the homeless beatings. Be in court for Jones's testimony. And he had to talk to Jones. Ask Jones? No. Tell Jones. Right. Tell Jones he was going to marry Lori. Ask Lori to marry him. Tell her, too? Deal with that later. He pulled his hair.

Still had to buy that ring. Or. He had his grandmother's. Would Lori want that? He tugged the hair between his kneading fingers. Didn't remember what the ring looked like. Or even where he had put it. Closet? In the cigar box?

Gibbs whistled, pulling him out of his musings. "Look at that." He was scrolling through Byron's data slowly. "He was the attorney of record for Burt Iverson."

Cav's turn to whistle. He'd read about the case. Iverson had been accused of murdering his wife and four of his children. The kids' bodies were missing. A fifth child, the youngest had been found unharmed. Byron believed Burt had been framed and investigated the brother-in-law, Peter. Found Peter had killed his sister and the oldest kid. Sold the other three. Byron located the kids who were reunited with their dad. "God, those kids must be in their thirties now. The brother thought he was going to get his sister's money."

"I recognize a few of these other cases, too," Ryan said pointing. "Same type of story. He really did defend the wrongfully accused." He moved to Max. Hit the highlights. "IRS agent for fifteen years, ending as a tax auditor examining corporate tax returns. Then she went into business for herself. Still submits a few tax returns for special clients."

"She's no dummy," Cav said.

"Mrs. Tubalt. Educator. Teacher and later principle of a parochial school. Another smart person."

"Huh," Cav said when Kingstone's bio came up.

"CID, U.S. Army Criminal Investigation Command. So, we can talk to both of them if we need to. Play it by ear."

*

Mrs. M opened the door at his first knock with her hand out. "Where's my badge?"

"Dollar Store special." He held up a badge, a five-pointed star with little crystals on the points. He handed it over. She held it in her palm, running a finger over the gems and smirked. Pinned it on.

Cav made introductions. "Maxine Mansard, this is Special Agent Ryan Gibbs. Gibbs, this is Mrs. Maxine Mansard."

She turned to Gibbs with her hand out again. "And my FBI badge?"

"I have a temporary loaner wallet, badge, and ID." He flipped the billfold open to show her.

"How temporary?"

"Until I can get you one to keep. This is an unusual process, but you are authorized as an agent of the FBI; the badge is not yours to keep, but the status is. Sort of a confidential informer/agent. It is highly unusual for us to give honorary status to people. In fact, I think only two or three people have been sworn in and received a badge. Elvis was one of them."

"It's good company I keep," she said.

"You are a real deputy sheriff, though," Cav told her. "I have the authority to do that."

"Come on in. I made coffee for us and tea for Agent Gibbs."

She settled them in the living room, pointed out the tray of food on the table, and went for coffee. Gibbs shook his head at Cav and walked to the wall of photographs.

Cav shrugged and headed to the food. "Being an astute investigator, I assume Lori told her you drink tea, though I imagine she can find out anything she wants to know on her own. She's scary." He studied a platter of sliders on the table. Looked like beef and ham. His mouth watered. Some had a green filling. Another platter had turnovers, cookies. Hmm. He checked his watch. Brunch? Paper plates, napkins, and silverware were set out beside the sandwiches. He was reaching for one, the meat, not the green, when Max came back with the drinks. Two coffees and a carafe, tea bags, and hot water. Sugar, cream, lemon, extra tea bags all arranged on a hand-painted tray.

"Sit, please," she said. "Help yourselves."

"Whatever we discuss here is confidential," Gibbs reminded her.

"Yes, I understand. I worked for the IRS. I understand confidential. Can you tell me about my car?"

Cav gave Gibbs an *I told you* so look and took the lead. He gave her some of what they knew about her car. "Someone has been using your car. We know where it is."

She didn't interrupt or ask questions, but her eyes hardened, and her lips flattened.

"The sheriff was able to pull a warrant to put the tracker on your car, but it would help if you signed this permission form for us." He handed it over and she signed it and handed it back.

"What about my house? Have you been in my house or talked to my neighbor?"

Gibbs answered, "No. We haven't been inside your house or talked to your neighbor. We don't want to alert anyone that we are interested."

He glanced over to Cav who asked, "Your database. Do you

know when these houses were vandalized? Or the types of damage? Were the police notified?"

"No. I would have included that information if I'd had it. I didn't feel that asking would be appropriate. You instructed me not to ask questions. I didn't know you were interested. You think the vandalisms are connected?" She scowled at both of them. "There's more to this than you're telling me. What is it? I'm a deputy, you can tell me."

Neither man responded. She frowned but said, "Well, if you want to know more, you should talk to my friend, Stone. Dennis Kingstone. He's lived here longer than me and knows everyone and everything. And he knows how to keep a confidence."

Gibbs nodded to Cav. "What can you tell me about Kingstone?"

"He didn't take my car."

"Correct. He is not involved with your car. What do you know about him?"

She stared at him. "Why?"

Cav replied, "Be nice to know a little about him, if we want him to help us with a problem."

She frowned. "That's not much of an answer, but I guess it's the best I'll get." She picked up a sandwich, reminding Cav they were there, and he grabbed a slider and took a bite before he realized he had a green one and almost choked. He swallowed. It wasn't too bad.

"I like him and I'm a good judge of character. He's fair and honest. Honorable. Treats people with respect. Residents and staff. Everyone. That's always a good sign."

She faced them both directly, daring them to make a comment. When neither did, she continued. "I don't know what else to tell you. He still owns his farm. He's on my spreadsheet. Has a property management company taking care of it. He doesn't go out there. He has no relatives except for one grandchild, who wants him to sell it and spend the money."

She seemed to notice the slider in her hand and took a bite.

"So no one lives in his house?"

"No"

"He go anywhere? Travel?"

"Sometimes he visits the granddaughter."

"Is that unusual?"

"I don't think so. I haven't been here long enough myself to know."

"Do you think he would talk to us?"

"Yes."

"Can you ask him if he'll come visit?"

"Will you tell me why?"

They exchanged another look. "Why don't you invite him for tea. Let us meet him. If we feel we can work with him, we'll explain to both of you what we know. Fair?"

She considered them. "You conned me, didn't you? I don't believe I let you do that. Asked me questions, I couldn't answer so I'd suggest you talk to Stone. You planned to speak to him all along. In fact, probably came here with that intention."

Cav played innocent. "I don't know what you mean."

"You know exactly what I mean. That's why you came with him," she said to Gibbs, then added. "Nicely done."

Gibbs also looked at her in innocent puzzlement. "It would be nice to meet the man."

She pulled out her cell and called Kingstone. "Come on over for tea sandwiches and meet Lori's young man." She pushed end and said, "He'll be right here; he's just down the hall."

Kingstone wasn't what Cav expected. Didn't look a day over sixty-five, had dark gray hair, not white. Wore a blue Guayabera hiding a small paunch. Blue jeans. Slippers on bare feet. Happy. Jovial. Greeted them both with a smile when Max introduced them. "So you fellas are Lori's friends? Just came over to visit Max?"

"Yeah," Cav said. "Just felt like it was time to meet some of Lori's friends."

Stone settled by Max, helping himself to a green slider while she poured him coffee. Took a bite of the sandwich. Swallowed and washed it down with some coffee. Snorted. "Well. Mr. Cavanaugh."

"Cav, call me Cav."

"Cav, then. And Ryan?"

"Ryan or Gibbs. I answer to both."

"Okay. It's interesting that two law enforcement guys feel a need to meet me. Have I done something wrong?"

Max smirked.

Cav pulled the hair at the back of his neck. He might be out of his depth with these older folks.

Gibbs laughed out loud. "Didn't really think we would fool you with that line. In fact, I'm pleased we didn't. We have a problem we'd like to share with the two of you, but first we need to ask some questions. Can you bear with us?"

Stone nodded. Took another bite. "Ask away."

"Well, we are particularly interested in anyone who lives here and still has a home which is unoccupied. Or maybe a property which has sustained damage."

Stone studied them. "Why?"

"Can you help us? Please? Then we'll answer questions." Gibbs waited.

Stone looked from one to the other. Cav grabbed a slider. Stone turned to Max and she said, "I already tried asking questions. It didn't work. Best to go along with them before they get out the rubber hoses."

Gibbs almost hid a grin. Cav half choked on a mouthful.

Stone smiled. "Okay let me think. Owns their own home which is vacant. No family members living in it?" he asked.

"Correct," Gibbs replied. "Empty."

Stone scratched his jaw. "There'd be Stella. Stella Novack. I drove her home one day. Just so she could look. I have my truck, she wanted to go walk through her house. Thinking of moving back.

Wanted to touch some stuff. The back door had been busted in and everything of monetary value was gone. She was devastated. But the robbers hadn't damaged or destroyed anything. The cops said they often destroy what they don't take so she felt lucky. Decided not to move back yet. Afraid someone would break in when she was home alone, don't you know."

He shook his head. "Poor thing. But she's doing well here. Sold the house as soon as she put it on the market. That the sort of thing you want?"

"Exactly. When was this?

"Oh, two, three months back."

"Remember the address?"

"Guess it's important, right?"

"Yes."

Stone pursed his lips, "Well then, Katy bar the door." He pulled out his cell. "Got it in here in my diary. He called up his calendar, read off the date. "Got the address, too." Read that off.

Cav stood and walked to the corner talking into his cell.

"Anyone else?"

Stone tipped his head. "Hearsay? Stella's the only one I know for a fact."

Gibbs smiled. "Hearsay is fine. Gossip will work too."

"Reggie Jones's place was broken into about, oh, a month later. Don't have that in here and I don't remember how he found out. Same situation as Stella. Address is out on White Boulevard, three thousand block, I think. Seem to remember it was almost the same number as mine. Don't know if he sold or not. He still lives here."

"Anyone else?"

"Inez, over in 6B. She went to her place and couldn't get in. Everyone thought she had the wrong key. But turned out squatters had been living there for a while. Same story as Stella. Anything of value was gone." He fiddled with his phone and read off the address. "Oh. Um, fire. Mr. Johnston's house burned. Last month. And I heard Mike Stavro's house was pretty well wrecked inside. Cops thought it might be, um, kids. Ripped out wiring and plasterboard. Cardboard boxes and cement blocks left inside."

Cav pulled his hair. Gibbs frowned.

"It's not coincidence is it? I never put the incidents together before. Seeing them laid out like this… Someone is targeting us. Or rather our empty homes?"

"Looks that way. Here is Max's list." He handed over an abbreviated version of Max's database to Stone.

Stone read it and whistled. "Katy bar the door, I hadn't heard about those other two over at New Spring Retirement Center. You have already done a lot of investigation. This is a pretty extensive list. You know, thinking about it like this? there was a story going around when I first got out of the hospital. Some woman came here from the hospital in bad shape. Her family flew in, were going to stay in her house, but it burned down that day. Blake, her name was Blake. I never heard any more about it."

Cav went back to the corner with his cell, asked Jones to check fire records on the Blake property. "Look for arson," he said. Explained why. Wondered if the drug dealers were moving sites every month or two.

"Do I assume, since both Max and I are here and we both have empty houses, we have a problem?"

Gibbs said, "Both homes appear to be occupied. Ms. Tubalt's also."

"My home. My friends' homes. Trying to get us to sell? Doesn't make any sense. No way they could profit from that. Somebody trying to buy them cheap?" Stone asked.

"We don't think they're trying to buy the buildings."

"What do you think?"

Cav said, "At this stage, we are still collecting facts. We have the properties under surveillance. There is more than one thing going on. Max's house, we feel, is most likely not connected to yours or Ms.

Tubalt's. Whatever is happening there is coincidental." He turned to Max, "We've made initial contact with the woman who is living in your house with her husband and baby. She says the contractor, the man building their new home, is having trouble getting their occupancy permit. He's letting them live rent free in your house. The woman appears innocent. The contractor also comes across as honest. No outstanding warrants and he has a good reputation. We think it's exactly what it looks like. The person we want is the one who rented your house to the contractor, Max. Your neighbor is watching your home, correct?"

"Yes. Mrs. Weldon. She's lived next door for twenty years. We traded keys ages ago and look out for each other. She would never do this. Rent out my house. Never."

He nodded. "Maybe not her, but I'm getting ahead of myself. We are going to hold off on confronting her. Would that be okay with you?"

"I'm nervous having strange people in my house. I don't like the idea, but I don't see how a few more days would make a difference. They can stay until you settle this mess."

"Good. The car is a different story. We can prove your car was used in multiple armed robberies."

"Oh, my goodness." Max put her hand to her chest. Stone reached out for her other hand.

"We have the vehicle under surveillance and expect we will be able to catch the thieves this weekend. Now tell me about your neighbor, Mrs. Weldon. Does she live alone?"

"Her nephew sometimes stays with her. Between incarcerations. It's him. Got to be. She would never let anyone stay in my house without talking to me," she said, anger wrinkling her mouth.

"What's his name," Cav asked pulling out his cell again. Why did he even put it away?

"Donny Edwards. He's a wrong one. Always in trouble. Always has an excuse or someone else to blame. She always buys it. It's embarrassing to watch how easily he manipulates her, but he is the spitting image of her husband at that age, and she is powerless to resist."

"Okay. Excuse me," Cav stood and walked away to call it in.

Gibbs took over the questions. "Mr. Kingstone."

"Call me, Stone."

"Stone. When are you moving back to your farm?"

"To tell the truth, I don't want to go back to the farm. That's my old life. I've started a new life here. I'm happy and well taken care of. Have lots of friends." He glanced at Max when he said friends. "My granddaughter wants me to sell it and spend the money on myself. But I don't need anything, so I've put it off. But soon. I'll sell soon."

"Who would know that you are not moving back?"

"Well, I haven't really told anyone. When I first came here, I thought it was the last stop. I couldn't take care of myself and needed nursing care."

"I'm sorry. How long ago was that?"

"Four months."

"You don't mind me saying, you look pretty healthy."

"I am. Now. The doctors said I had a large tumor in my lungs. They gave me two months at most. A thirty-five percent chance of surviving surgery. I was here for about a month. To tell you the truth, I wasn't paying attention to much of anything but my next breath. We decided to do an exploratory. They opened me up and found, not cancer, but a growth around a tiny stainless-steel sliver that had somehow become embedded in my lung. They removed the mass and one week later I was up and walking and jogging. By then I'd decided I liked it here." He moved his eyes toward Max. "Liked the people."

"You have a property manager, correct?"

"Yes."

"As far as he knows, you are still dying?"

"Probably."

"Name?"

"Um, John Steward of Home Stewards. Kind of liked the play on words. And you can call me senile because it never occurred to me to check on him. Or my farm."

Cav headed back to the sliders. He grabbed his head. Wasn't pulling on his hair. Just rubbing his neck.

Stone sighed and shook his head. "Truth. I just didn't want to think about it. Guess they count on that."

This time Max reached for Stone's hand. Yup, Cav thought, some hanky-panky going on at the retirement facility. He exchanged a look with Gibbs.

"That it?" Stone asked. "That the connection? They're the ones doing this?"

Cav hedged. "Too early to make that determination. Might you have told anyone about Stewards? That you use them?"

Stone stopped short. "Yes. Like people told Max."

"Anyone in particular?"

Stone thought, then frowned. "No. In a group. People coming and going and we were talking about life before. You think someone here?"

Gibbs stood. "We don't want to jump to conclusions; the Forest connection is one avenue we will examine."

Stone accepted that. "Okay. For now. But I want—both of us want—to be kept in the loop."

"As much as possible. There are things we can't say, though. Now we need a reason for Cav and I to be here today in case anyone asks."

"You were here for some tax help. Confidential tax help for my unidentified client. Though I may let it slip that you are in bad trouble with the IRS."

Gibbs laughed. "Ouch. You folks have been very helpful. I can't emphasize enough that you don't share any of this. It is a highly sensitive investigation. Do nothing, say nothing. If you hear anything, give one of us a call." Both Gibbs and Cav handed over cards.

Cav snatched two sliders on their way out. "Stewards might be a little iffy. We're doing a deeper check."

"Too easy," Gibbs said.

"Easy's okay."

"Does not happen often though." Gibbs frowned. "I need to talk to Dawson personally. Make sure he understands what I mean by working together. And I'll meet with Dylan, have him contact Jones."

"I'm heading for court. I'll check Stewards," Cav said.

*

Cav slipped into the courtroom just as the defense attorney started with Jones. "Yes, we were pretty lucky, sir," Jones agreed with the attorney. "I mean we were lucky she was home when we went back to re-interview the neighbors."

"This was months after the incident, right? You really expect the jury to believe that you found a new witness, months after the incident?"

"Yes sir. She wasn't interviewed originally because she was out of town."

"Left town right after the incident, officer?"

"No sir. She wasn't home the night the house exploded sir."

"She wasn't home that night." The defense attorney turned a puzzled face to the jury. "The witness wasn't home the night of the incident." He turned back to Jones. "Then how could she say she saw my client? Is she psychic?"

The jury laughed.

"Oh no sir, she didn't say that sir. She said she'd seen the defendant around the house many times since the bank foreclosed on his family last year."

"She did not see my client that night."

"No, sir. She didn't, but her information gave us the lead that led us directly to his truck. That type and color truck was seen racing away from the scene. That truck had outstanding warrants. And we found his fingerprints at the scene."

"Well surely if he lived in that house his prints would be inside."

"Yes, sir, I agree. But we found his prints on the plastic covering the windows. We also," Jones hurried on, "found his prints on empty containers of antifreeze and ether, both used to cook methamphetamine, which the fire department said was the cause of the explosion. We found where he bought his supplies. He charged them to his father's credit card."

Jones smiled at him. The jury smiled with him.

The attorney looked like he wished he had never asked that question.

"We talked to his buddy and the buddy rolled," Jones continued. "Admitted the whole thing."

Cav was smiling when he left the courthouse with Jones, glad he'd made the time to attend. "You did a good job up there," he told Jones.

"Seemed pretty easy, Sir."

"Don't use sir on me. You reserve that for defense attorneys," Cav warned him.

Jones laughed at him. "Yes, Sheriff. Now I'm heading out to check on our surveillance vehicles."

"Gibbs will have a specialist contact you, by name of Dylan. And Gibbs will continue to work with DEA Agent in Charge Dawson to make sure we get the help we need, how we need it, and when we need it. He'll get back to us."

He went back to the office, updated Chavez on Gibbs and Jones.

"That kid has a good head on his shoulders," Chavez said. "It's time for you to promote him into that open detective slot. Past time if you ask me."

Cav did the hair thing, admitted, "There's a complication."

"If you mean you and his sister, no one is going to hold that against him. The kid earned his spot on his own merits."

Cav left his hand in his hair but did close his mouth. "What?"

"You and Jones's sister. No one cares."

Cav closed his eyes a moment. Opened them again to see Chavez laughing at him. "You think no one knows you're banging his sister?"

"Well, yeah. I kind of thought we had kept that quiet."

"This is a cop shop, boss. We're detectives. We probably knew about it before you did."

"And you're okay with it? The men are?"

"Yes, boss. Look. There's always going to be one or two complainers, but in this case the complaints are that you're not promoting Jones because of reverse favoritism. The kid is good, smart, tough. Shares collars. The men like him. Respect him."

Cav sat. Huh. "What happens. Um, what happens if it is more serious then banging?" He didn't like that term used to describe his relationship with Lori. It had never been 'just banging'.

"No one cares, boss. Just promote him. Your only worry is that he's going to be ready for your job soon." Chavez laughed at him, changed the subject. "The men will be ready to head out on the stakeout soon. It's all set up."

"Good. Get out of my office." Cav dealt with routine problems for the rest of the day and was between tasks when he heard Chavez exclaim, "God you people reek. What is that stink?"

Cav stepped out into the squad room and nearly choked. The stench was vile. He couldn't tell which of the four reeking homeless bums was the source. Three men and one woman. He thought.

The woman. It was the woman who stank the worst. He tried to make a wide berth around her, but the room was too small, and the reek reached the corners. He scrunched up his face and squeezed his nose between his thumb and forefinger.

"Man. What is that stuff?"

His men grinned. One said, "That's Sally. She won't tell us what it is. Says she's going to patent it as the newest fragrance. But she's definitely the winner of the foulest stench contest for this operation." He coughed. "Makes my eyes water. I think she outdid herself and I'm just glad she won't be anywhere near my location. Can't wait to get out into the fresh air."

Cav wanted them all out in the fresh air. And the windows opened.

He checked with Chavez. "Everyone know the plan? Got the unmarked cars in place?"

"All set boss. Just wanted you to see these guys," Chavez was trying not to laugh. Or breathe. Wasn't wimp enough to put his hand over his nose. "All right men, get out there and do your job. Get me that thug. And for goodness sake, don't touch anything on your way out."

With a chorus of yes sirs most of the stench went out the door.

Now Chavez did laugh. "Glad to see the rivalry for most disreputable, dirty, stinking homeless outfit still exists, but I sure am glad to have them gone. Let's leave the door open and air the place out."

"Yeah, but boy, that was truly bad." Cav was afraid Sally's fragrance might be etched in his nose. Hoped she'd be able to wash it off. "I'm not sure any of them should be allowed in an official vehicle." They'd decided that four cops disguised as beggars spread through the homeless section of town would be enough. His men, and woman, would be targets. Unmarked cars were parked close enough to rush in to help if anyone was attacked, cop or real beggar. If the thug followed his habit, they expected he would attack late this afternoon or tonight.

While he was gone, someone filled his inbox. He'd only stepped into the squad room for what, ten minutes? He sorted through it but couldn't really concentrate. Everyone knew? Did Kevin know? He shook his head. No. If Kevin knew he'd have made comments.

He pulled his hair one more time and forced himself to concentrate on work. That was the answer.

And an hour later, with nothing else needing his attention here at the office, he decided to prepare his reports at home. That thought brought him up short because the home he saw in his mind was Lori's. Was this the first time he'd thought of her condo as home? He didn't think so. Just the first time he noticed. It felt right. Home. And now that he thought of it, who was he kidding? He seldom spent the night at his place. Somehow it felt barren, empty, lonely. He'd been bringing work home to Lori's. When had that happened? She didn't mind when he sat at the counter with his laptop. Didn't ask to go out or demand attention. She did her own work and let him work. He was living with Lori. In her apartment. How had he not noticed? Then his mind jumped to, 'we'll need a bigger place. One large enough for kids.'

Huh? Where had that come from?

He'd just come to recognize the idea of love, accepted it, digested it, and already he was thinking home and two kids? The blue house would be perfect.

He laughed at himself. Right. The blue house.

He called Lori and volunteered to bring home supper. "I'll be bringing home paperwork I have to do," he said. "That okay?"

"Sure, I've got work too. Bring me some pork fried rice. See you in a bit."

Simple. He frowned, ordered dinner, and headed home. Home. With supper. Home. And, thankfully, Sally's fragrance was just a memory. A bad memory.

"Went over to Max's with Gibbs and met Stone today," Cav said over pork fried rice. "Stone had more information." He gave Lori the same abbreviated version of the case they had given Max and Stone, warned her not to speak of the investigation with anyone, including Max and Stone. "It's dangerous, and I don't want you three in the middle of it."

"I was afraid I was imagining things. Afraid I would be bothering you, that's why I went to look at the houses first."

"Looking at the houses was a reasonable action. Telling me, turning the matter over to a professional, was the logical next step."

"Becca told me to go to you when I told her. It is drugs isn't it?"

"Maybe," he said but stopped himself. This was Lori, and she'd brought the case to him. "Most likely. We think the Stone and Tubalt properties are drugs. Max's house is beginning to look like her neighbor or the neighbor's nephew took advantage of her being gone."

He paused, grimaced. "I can't tell you more just yet. Oh, if anyone asks, I took Gibbs with me today because he needed expert tax help." Cav paused to see if she understood and she laughed. "Right. Like Gibbs would try to cheat the IRS."

"Yeah, I liked it too."

He worked at the counter writing reports; she worked at the kitchen table summarizing her patient progress notes. He kept sneaking glances. Yep. They'd been doing this for a while now. Like a married couple. He caught her looking at him with her tongue between her lips.

Something still there.

"Hey." He tilted his head in a question and she shrugged a shoulder, gave him a half smile.

"Hey, back at ya,"

"Everything okay?" he asked giving her an opening.

"Just scheduling. You know how I hate it." She looked back down at her schedule, tongue still between her teeth.

Cav tugged at his hair; she wasn't ready to talk about it. And, apparently, he wasn't ready to talk about his thoughts either. "Interesting man, Stone." Safe topic.

"He's amazing. And a terrific match for Max. Both healthy, smart. I like them. They make a great couple." She said it with enthusiasm and a laugh. "I wonder if they'll get married or live together in sin." Her eyes crossed and she looked down at her paperwork.

He decided not to push. Give her another day.

His mind wandered. The new house maybe should have an office they could share. He wondered what the blue house looked like inside. Shook his head.

Made notes to himself on who he wanted on the team to take down the drug dealers, rearranging schedules, drawing up a plan for Gibbs in the morning. He'd give Eggert one more day to show up. Humph. Needed a plan for that. Take him down? Follow him?

Take him down. Leave the Estates house open as their mousetrap, follow the buyers, take down the ones they had under surveillance. Take them on their home turf and bust their sell houses. Keep watch on the farm and Estates house. Or just hit them all at the same time. There should be plenty of manpower with the FBI and DEA assistance. He did as much as he could before talking with DEA.

When he finished, they settled together on the couch with popcorn to watch a movie. Like an old married couple.

His cell buzzed right before the ending of the show. Chavez. He stood to take it in the kitchen.

"Boss, we may have a problem," Chavez said.

"Where? When? What?" he asked.

"Sally. Um Sally put the guy in the hospital."

"What guy? How? Is she okay?"

It took ten minutes for Chavez to explain, and the final credits were rolling when he got back to the couch.

"Want to know the ending?" Lori asked.

"The good guy got the girl?" Cav guessed.

"You got it in one." She nodded at the phone, "Everything okay?"

"Yeah. We got the guy who has been beating up the vagrants. But there are some complications. I have to go," he said as he strapped on his weapon, kissed her goodbye, and headed out. "Love you."

"Um. I'll leave the light on."

Um?

Cav walked into the emergency room entrance as the hazmat team was just leaving. "Everything's clear Chief," their leader said, "only pepper spray. We're heading home."

"Thanks, guys." Cav turned to Chavez. "Okay, tell me how this went down."

"I was making my rounds, keeping an eye on our decoys. Just as I rounded the corner, I saw a guy sneak up to Sally. Screaming at her he aimed a baseball bat at her head. Got in a glancing blow, but she was already rolling away. He swung at her again and she yelled, 'Police, stop!' and rolled out of range. He charged and swung again, and she kicked his arm. He dropped the bat and tried to kick her in the ribs. She tripped him. He pulled a can from his pocket and pointed it toward her face, and she grabbed his arm as they struggled. She twisted his arm around. He pulled the trigger and sprayed himself in the face. She got some blowback mist. We used Sudecon Decontamination Wipes. Called Hazmat. They diagnosed pepper spray. Doctors confirm it."

Sally came out of a cubicle with a huge grin on her red face. Eyes still running.

"Tell me what happened," Cav instructed.

"The guy came running at me, yelling. I heard him, of course. Forewarned. Looked up to see this big dude race up and try to hit me in the head with a baseball bat. But I was ready and moving. Dodged the blow, mostly." She pointed to a bruise forming on her cheek. "It stunned me a moment. He tried again and I screamed, 'Police. Stop.' I kicked his arm and he dropped the bat and, swearing, brought up something and aimed it at my head. I grabbed his hand and we struggled. I had his arm twisted, but he sprayed the canister at me. Got himself in the face. I got some blowback."

She pointed at her face and stopped her hand before she wiped her eyes.

She took a breath. "Pepper spray canister sir. I heard yelling. For a second, I thought it was me and tried to stop, but I was coughing too hard and the screaming continued. I squeezed my eyes and tried to see through the spray. It was the guy yelling. Wiping his face frantically. His shrieking morphed into words. He was screaming that I'd burned him. 'You burned me. You burned me. Oh it hurts. It hurts,' he said. I mean the guy was crying. Seriously, he kicks me, hits me in the head with a bat, and tries to pepper spray me, and he's crying I hurt him?" She took a breath and wiped at her face.

"Chavez was there by then. We threw him on his stomach and cuffed his hands behind his back. The creep's face was all red and starting to blister. We didn't know what it was then, so we called Hazmat and I stripped out of my costume."

She coughed. "Hazmat hosed us both down. We took the perp to the hospital and he's fine. I'm sorry that he was hurt. My body cam was on the whole time, Sir."

Sally's face was bright red, and Cav wasn't sure if the color was from the chemicals or excitement.

"You're okay?"

"Eyes still sting. Nothing worse than in training."

Sure. Because trainees all learned how it felt to be pepper sprayed. And how to work through the reactions. She'd done well. "Okay. Good job. Go with Chavez, give him your statement, fill out your reports, go home, get some rest. I'll see you tomorrow at the start of your shift." He'd almost told her to go home and do the reports in the morning, but she was bouncing off the walls with energy. Filling out reports and answering questions would bring her down quick enough.

He watched them go and went in search of the mugger. Found him being wheeled to his room, his head bandaged, and handcuffed to the bed with two cops following. He gave his men a nod. "You're on him until you're relieved. I want to know if he has visitors, and he's not to be alone at any time."

"Got it Boss. Not alone with anyone, except his attorney?"

Cav grimaced. "Right." They followed behind the thug.

Cav hung back and asked the doctor the crook's status.

"We had to give him a sedative. Kept screaming the cop burned him. Crying like a baby. Like he was really hurt. The guy was hysterical." The doctor shook his head. "Guy didn't have any injuries, just the pepper spray. We checked him over because he claimed he was hurt and in great pain. And because of his accusations. He claimed your cop punched him. Hit him with his baton. Burned his face and hands. Did it because he was slow getting out his ID. He's going to the media and tell them about police brutality, and he wanted me to tell him the cop's name. I didn't know, so I couldn't. Wouldn't have anyhow."

Shook his head again. "He wasn't battered or bruised. We took photos. No signs of him being hit or mistreated. Just pepper sprayed. Said he saw the cop's face. And he knows the cop came into emergency for treatment, his attorney will find him."

The doctor scowled. "He couldn't stop crying. I saw your cop, she was pretty messed up herself, but took it like a trooper. No whimpering or moaning like this guy. Glad you sent her away, though; she stank real bad. Even the shower didn't help much. Sure looked like a homeless person."

Cav laughed. "Yep. She's a good cop. My men will stay with the suspect until he's transferred to the lockup."

Lori was asleep when he rolled into bed beside her and pulled her close. Laid a gentle kiss on the back of her neck. Love you, he thought and fell asleep with a smile in his heart.

# THURSDAY

Cav read through the statements Sally and Chavez had completed; another cop would interview the two later today. Then he watched Sally's bodycam footage along with Chavez's. Everything supported the written statements and the verbal reports he'd heard last night. He hadn't expected anything different. He put them aside and worked his way through his inbox, humming. Nothing like wakeup sex to put a guy in a good mood. Not even the full inbox which he had emptied last night. He'd tried out the love word again, Lori hadn't seemed to notice.

He stopped what he was doing to consider that, and the glow came off. Maybe she was still planning to dump him. She couldn't. She loved him. He knew she did. So what wasn't she telling him. He tossed that thought around for a while, but couldn't come up with an answer. Something there. He was sure of it. But how to get her to tell. He'd ponder it. Yes. That's what he'd do. Ponder it.

His pondering was interrupted by his secretary. "We're getting killed on the news and on social media," she said as she turned on his TV and the news.

"My client, Tom Russo, has been beaten by the police. Unlawfully detained. All because he took a walk." The attorney held up a photo of his client, Cav's thug, with a swollen red face. And cuts and bruises. "This is what they did to him because he was a little slow getting his ID out of his wallet. This is clearly a case of police brutality. My client has identified the cop and we've ascertained his name is S. Stanton. This brute is out on the streets walking around looking for some other poor unfortunate to beat half to death. He should be in jail. Do you hear that Mr. Mayor, Mr. DA? I challenge you to get this violent cop off the streets."

Cav's phones were ringing, and he muted the TV. "That will be the DA or the Mayor." He picked up the phone and began talking, didn't much matter which one it was, he knew what they were going to say. "My cop had the camcorder on all the time. It clearly depicts Mr. Tom L. Russo trying to kick a homeless vagrant and beat him in the head with a bat. Russo's face is red because when he tried to use mace on my cop, he got hit with it."

There was a long silence on the other end of the line. "We're on our way over. This isn't going to be allowed. Tell your cop to present himself in dress uniform for our news conference."

His call caught Sally as she was walking out the door. "Wear your dress uniform." He explained.

"Boss," she almost whined. "Don't make me do this."

"The Mayor is making you do this. Making both of us do this. Do what I do. Answer yes or no to any reasonable question. Frown at the camera, grunt to stupid questions." He thought about that. "No, don't frown. I mean, unless they ask you something stupid. Be yourself. You'll be okay. Chavez will be with you. He can frown." Chavez's frown would stop anyone cold.

"Any idea how the creep was injured?" he asked her.

"We didn't do it, honest boss."

"I know that. The question was do you know how it happened."

"Oh yeah. In the emergency room. He beat his head against the wall. We had to help the orderlies pull him away from it and—"

Cav smiled and finished the statement. "And there will be video, because the emergency room has multiple cameras."

Cav called in his secretary. "Call down to the emergency room.

Get their video from last night. We'll need it for the press conference. Please." He called Chavez next. Told him, dress uniform. He didn't have to tell Chavez to frown, that came naturally to him.

Better take his own advice and go home and get his own dress uniform, he thought. Home. He chuckled to himself. Lori's place was home. Not his place, and he had a nice place. Lori's condo was home. Because she was there.

Her car was in her assigned parking spot. Had she told him she'd be home this morning? No. He pulled his hair. Rubbed his left index knuckle against his teeth. Caught himself doing that. Grimaced. Both signals of unease. His tells. Why was she home? There could be lots of good reasons. He knew that. But he couldn't stop the fleeting thought that he'd catch her with another man. Shook his head. He felt guilty for even thinking it for a moment. Having that dirty little thought in the dark corner of his mind made him make a lot of noise as he took out his keys and opened the door. He'd been a cop for a long time and seen the worst in people. She'd never do that. Never. Sneak around behind his back. Take another lover when she was still involved with him. She was too honest. Too true. And she loved him. He knew she did.

"Honey, I'm home," he called as he walked into the kitchen where she was shuffling papers at the table. Not just shuffling, burying some with a guilty motion. Not another man, something else.

She jumped up and hugged him, giving him a kiss.

"Mmmm. We have to meet like this more often," he murmured.

She pulled back. "How are you? I saw the news. It's awful. What are you going to do?"

"Change into my dress uniform for a command performance at a press conference with the mayor and the D.A.

"Are they throwing you to the wolves?"

"No. We are going to share our body cam videos of the man attacking my officer. It's the attorney and his client who are going down. What about you?" he asked, heading for the bedroom. "How come you're home?"

He didn't see her hesitate before answering. "Had a break and decided to come home and catch up on paperwork. Have lunch here."

"Wish I could join you," he called as he unpinned his badge and unbuckled his belt and laid them on the bed. Toed off his boots and pulled off his clothes, folding them neatly over the chair.

She walked to the doorway. "Yeah. Maybe we should schedule an assignation, midday. Would be fun. You really have video of that guy attacking Sally?"

He pulled on his shirt. "Oh, yeah. Two views. Sally's body cam and Chavez's. This is almost going to be fun." He buttoned his shirt and added the badge.

"Why almost?"

"Because there will always be those people who heard the villain's version or choose to believe his version. People like to remember the bad stuff. There will always be that little tarnish." He pulled on his pants and added his equipment belt. Sat and pulled on his boots. "On the other hand. Folks just love video." Checked his watch. He grabbed her in for a kiss. "Let's make that assignation plan tonight. Gotta go. Love you."

The *l* word slipped out again. "I mean that. I love you. This isn't quite the way I planned to tell you. Another thing we should discuss tonight." He waited, but she didn't respond. He kissed her again and was out the door.

Damn, he thought, angry at himself for the way he'd told her. He bit his lip, because she hadn't replied. What did that mean? Disturbed still about his moment of distrust, it seemed like the second time, in what, two days? He didn't like the way it made him feel. Guilty. Grimy. But she was keeping a secret. Had hidden paperwork. Papers she didn't want him to see. Hadn't said she loved him. He caught himself reaching up to pull his hair. They'd talk tonight.

His cell rang as he was approaching the station, the back entrance, because media trucks already had the road blocked out front.

It was Gibbs.

"Tell me some good news. What have you got?"

"Meeting this afternoon. FBI, DEA, Staties from all four states and the district. DEA has a guy, a specialist in coordination who will be there. You and Jones are included. We'll be going over the timeline. And thanks for delegating Jones."

Cav nodded. "So, am I going to like the timeline?"

"Meets your requirements. So, yes. Jones outlined your conditions quite eloquently. Very convincing. He found a lot of agreement in the group. Of course, the fact he said you are going in tomorrow to shut down the drug operation helped." Gibbs laughed. "You going to be able to make the meet? You guys are being hammered by the media. Any truth in there?"

"Hah. Protesters are picketing in front of the station. Demanding we prosecute the cop who beat up the innocent man who was just walking home. Where did they come from? How did they get to the station so quickly? Why?"

"Are those rhetorical questions?" Gibbs asked. "I don't have the answers. Maybe someone should do a study. Interview them. Don't you know? Cops and doctors are not allowed to make a mistake. At least you don't have a deadly result. Your perp is still among the living."

"We didn't make a mistake. Watch us in—" he looked at his watch—"fifteen minutes. See it live."

He found Sally a bundle of nerves. Standing at attention. She begged, "Sir. Please don't make me do this."

"I'm not making you do this. The Mayor is making us do this."

"Please, Sir. Let me go home. You don't need me. Just show my body cam video."

"Stop."

"Yes, Sir."

"Don't call me sir."

"Yes, Sir." Still at attention, her hands continued shaking.

"Where is that tough cop who was in the office last night. That smug stinky one. Where's the cop who took down the thug trying to batter a helpless victim with a baseball bat?"

"I'm here Sir, but—"

"Don't call me sir. And stop standing at attention. Man up. I expect better of you."

Some of her stiffness melted at the insult.

"Please Sir, um Boss. Can't you do this without me?"

"No. I have to be there. Chavez has to be there. Look at him." Chavez was standing calmly stoic. "He doesn't want to be there either." Cav pointed with his chin. "Go sit on the floor against that wall."

"What?"

"You heard me. Sit over there and assume the same position you were in when that thug attacked you. Can you do that?"

With a puzzled look she followed his order.

"Now report. Tell me how it happened. That guy is coming at you. What did you do? Did you have any choice in your reaction? Would you have done anything differently?"

"Um. I could have leaned out of the way."

"The video shows you leaned out of the way. Anything else you could have done?"

"No, Sir."

"No what?"

"No Boss." She was calmer now. A cop making a report. He made her demonstrate each step. She walked him through it. Then he summarized. "He attacked you with a bat, kicked you. You leaned out of the way while warding off the blow which caught you on the cheek. He came at you again and you disarmed him, identified yourself. Chavez came running in, identifying himself. The perp pulled out his pepper spray, and you swiped his arm ruining his aim, but you both catch some. You bring him down while he's screaming from the pepper. Chavez gets to you and the both of you roll him over, handcuff him. Is that what happened? Is that what you wrote in your report? Does Chavez's report back you up? Do your bodycams back you up?"

"Yes," she said.

"Now I want to hear you repeat that to me. Just like you did at the hospital last night."

She did, a little hesitantly at first, but finished up in a strong, determined tone.

"Okay. That's what I want to hear at the press conference. That tough cop we all know. Not that wimpy sister act you've been putting on this morning. Am I clear?"

"Yes, Boss. No problem." She smiled, relaxed. All hard cop.

"And don't smile. Frown like Chavez."

"Yes, Sir. I mean, no, I won't."

Chavez gave him a thumbs-up. The mayor and DA came in and they headed into the conference room full of rowdy media. The mayor pushed Cav to the podium.

He waited until the media got tired of screaming out questions and demands for the cop to be fired. Then spoke so quietly, they had to strain to hear.

"I'm going to show you some videos and then make a statement." He nodded to the IT guy. The reporters watched. He heard gasps when the bat was swung toward the body cam and positive comments at the end of the first video. 'Gut the bastard' was one of them. IT immediately ran Chavez's without a break, so the audience saw the action from two points of view.

During the second video, Cav's cell buzzed an incoming text. He reached for it surreptitiously, saw Chavez do the same.

"Sergeant Chavez took the second video. Any comments Sergeant?'

"I'll let the video speak for itself."

The attorney rushed up. "So where is the bodycam footage of your cop beating my client. And where is he. He too chicken to show his face?"

The audience picked up the theme and Cav looked out at the reporters and waited for quiet.

"Both cops are here."

"Where?" the attorney screamed with a sneer and turned to smile at the reporters. "You see another cop?"

Angry murmurs rose from the crowd.

Cav nodded to Chavez to leave and waited for silence again. Didn't take long. The group was trainable. "The brute is here behind me and will welcome questions in a moment. There are no police videos of a beating, but we do have one from the emergency room." He motioned to the two 10x10 monitors and they watched the hospital video of Russo beating his head bloody against the wall. Cops helping EMTs drag the guy out of the room with blood spraying from his wounds.

He turned to Sally, winked. "Officer Stanton will take questions."

She was clearly not what they expected, and a stunned silence was followed quickly by shouted questions. He'd told her to select the ones she wanted to answer and ignore the rest. No one would notice because a dozen different questions would be screamed at her at a time. She chose "You're the cop in the video, Officer Stanton?"

Cav stepped back.

"Yes. Sir," Sally replied with a small smile. Her 'screw you' smile. The reporter would never know he was being dished.

Cav gave the media five minutes with her. Watched as she had them eating out of her hand. Cav had given them gruff and curt;

she gave them sweet one-word answers with a smile. Except when she said with sincere apology, "I'm sorry I can't answer that." She was in her zone and could handle the mob. He smiled to himself as he pulled her out, walked her to the office, sat her in a chair and brought her coffee and a donut. She wanted jelly filled. Forget about Jones, he thought, it would be Sally after his job in a few years.

Jones was waiting in the office. "The puddle jumper is on the move?" Cav asked him while doing another strip. "It's not Friday." He took off his dress shirt and pulled on a sweaty t-shirt he kept in his gym duffle. Left on the pants, kept the holster on his belt.

"Not Friday, but it is the end of the month. Monthly payroll at the toy factory. Today. Over seven hundred people get their checks at four. Plus, bonus checks today, too. And they all head for two check cashing shops. Either Quick Check Cashing or Payday Loans. They get their cash, and a number don't come back to work."

"Who'd a thunk." Cav pulled his running shoes on. Might need them.

"The two shops are about a block apart. Chavez is on his way along with a second unmarked. Our people will be inside both when the puddle jumper gets there."

"We're following the GPS?" Cav asked.

"Oh, yeah. Don't want to make a mistake like waiting at the wrong store. Two more vehicles are ready to follow us."

"Okay. I'll drive my truck, you navigate. Quick Check is on the corner at West and Main?"

"Yeah. Payday is mid-block on Main."

"How did you find out about the payroll? Wait, I know. You did a search on our arrest records for peaks in call outs and arrests."

"Right. Had a lot of free time while sitting on those two properties. Found a number of incidents tied to payroll check cashing. It's something we should look at. Got a couple of bi-weekly paydays too. Less money then, though."

Cav was nodding to himself. The kid was sharp. Deserved the

promotion. Hell. He deserved to have the kid in a management position. But he'd have to stop thinking of him as the kid.

They were almost to Main when Jones said, "He's stopped." Then in a thoughtful tone, he added, "Parking midway between both shops."

They looked at each other. "He's going to hit them both."

Cav made the turn onto Main, slowed as he went by Payday.

"Can't see inside," Jones said. "There's the car."

Cav cruised by, looking for a parking spot. Jones kept his head down. "Two men in the car. Can't tell if one is Donny Edwards." Max's neighbor, Mrs. Weldon's nephew.

"Four men in the other robberies," Cav said. Who said he couldn't add? So where were the other two? No way to identify any of them. Donny was the only one they knew.

Chavez was standing in front of Quick Check, leaning against the door jamb, smoking.

"I'm making a U-turn and parking across the street. We can get out and study that map on the hood."

"Uh-oh," Jones said.

"What?"

"That red truck that just pulled in near Payday? That was in the construction parking lot with the puddle jumper. No mistaking that truck." They both got out of the vehicle and walked to the hood. Cav spread out a map. Who used maps anymore anyhow? "Two men in the truck."

The two men stepped down from the truck. Nodded to the two who got out of the puddle-jumper. All four wore red plaid shirts and black baseball caps pulled low. Donny and his partner headed for Quick Check. The other two, one carrying a hard-shell pool cue stick case, the other a soft sided case, went into Payday. A 'closed' sign appeared in the window.

Chavez, a glance to Cav, tossed his cigarette aside and followed right behind Donny.

Cav and Jones headed for Payday. No communication needed. Chavez could handle Quick Check. But the cops in Payday would be waiting for Donny. Not two unknown robbers.

Cav tried them by phone. No answer. He braced the phone between his left shoulder and ear, pushed the door open with his left hand. Took four steps inside while speaking on the phone. Not hearing the redshirt man yelling at him, "The shop's closed, dipshit. Didn't you see the sign?" Didn't notice the rifle pointing at the customers lined up at the counter. Or the revolver aimed at the cashier in the cage. Cav was intensely involved in a conversation on his cell, his eyes only on the floor. He waved his left hand uselessly around, showing he was busy on the phone and couldn't be bothered with whatever the guy was shouting. Jones glided by him and near the crook by the register. Cav watched feet and took a step to the left and finally looked up at the man yelling at him.

His eyes widened as he took in the rifle "What? What the fuck?"

The rifle barrel swung toward him. Counted on that, Cav thought, grabbed the barrel. Pushed it down and pulled the man off balance.

Jones shoved his weapon into the other guy's neck. "Police," he said, "drop it."

Cav used his leverage on the gun barrel to force the guy down, yelled, "Stay down, on your knees. Police. Everyone stay where you are."

The cops in the shop cuffed both crooks. "Sorry, sir. We were looking for Edwards."

"Yeah. We figured that. Jones recognized these two and we followed them in. Read 'em their rights." He looked around the shop. "Everyone okay?" He could see they were but had to ask and waited for nods from the three customers and two employees.

Squad cars pulled up out front. Filled the street. Uniformed men spilled into the shop. Cav asked, "What's happening in Quick Check Cashing?"

"Chavez requested transport for two prisoners. Two squad cars have them."

"Take these two in also; keep them all separated."

While his men took statements from the customers and workers, he checked in with Chavez and headed back to the office.

He made Donny and his three buddies wait for an hour in holding and then had them brought to separate interrogation rooms. Looked them all over. Started with Donny.

"Mr. Edwards," he said as he walked in.

"Not talking without my lawyer. I haven't had my phone call yet."

"Do you want to talk before he gets here? Maybe make a deal?"

Donny smirked at him. "Phone call. I've been here before. Not talking."

"Okay." Cav nodded to the cop to give Donny a phone and left.

"Always a chance a guy will be an idiot, but he's been here before, knows the ropes," Cav said to Jones as he walked to the room holding Carlson, the robber he had disarmed. As he opened the door to interrogation room six, he stopped in the doorway as if to finish a thought. "No. Jones. Whenever someone dies during a crime the law says its murder. And everyone committing the crime can be punished by death. Doesn't matter who pulled the trigger. Doesn't matter if the victim dies of a heart attack. It's murder during the commission of a crime. Everyone gets punished."

"Doesn't seem fair, Sir," Jones said quickly picking up and expanding on the idea. "I know it's the law, but sometimes the D.A. will cut a deal with one of the crooks, right? Like if he testifies against his partners? He doesn't get the death penalty, right?"

"Yeah. That happens. Makes it easier to get a conviction against the murderer and is fairer to the quote, innocent crook, unquote."

Carlson was licking his upper lip and tapping the fingers of his right hand on the tabletop. Nervous. Just what Cav had been hoping for. Chavez and Detective Harry Coleman were sitting with

Carlson. "Mr. Jack Carlson, I don't believe I introduced myself ear-lier. I'm Sheriff Cavanaugh. This is Deputy Jones. Can we talk for a few minutes?"

Carlson's eyes shifted from Cav to Chavez, to Coleman. Shook his head.

"Does that mean no?"

"Ahh. Talk about what. We didn't shoot anyone."

"I know that. Can we talk?"

"Don't I need a lawyer?"

"Up to you. I just wanted to go over a few points with you, see if we could come up with a compromise. But if you want an attorney, that's your right."

"I don't have one."

"We'll get one for you We did read you your rights at Payday when we took your gun away from you in the middle of an armed robbery. We'll leave now if you want your attorney. But we won't be able to talk about a deal then."

Carlson licked his lips again. "I didn't shoot anyone. You were there. You know."

Cav sat and leaned back, relaxed in his chair. Chavez did the same. Coleman chose to lean against the door frame. "No one was shot at Payday." Cav displayed his puzzled face. "Oh, you heard that discussion as we came into the room. Nothing to do with you. How about you help me fill in some gaps in our information. You know, so we can complete our reports. We won't talk about any shooting without an attorney. Okay?" Cav was using his best stern but sup-portive favorite uncle impression.

Carlson licked his lips. "Ah. No. No, I don't need an attorney for that."

"Okay. But I'm going to read you your rights again because I am required to, and you will have to sign a form waiving your right to an attorney. The whole process will be recorded."

When Carlson signed the waiver, Cav looked down at his

paperwork and asked, "How did you meet Mr. Moore? Mr. John Thomas Moore?" Carlson's partner in the robbery.

Carlson was tapping both hands softly on the table

"Um. At work. We're both day laborers. It's good work, you know and Mr. Newton, our boss, he's a good guy. We worked together and, then one day, went for a beer together. Kind of got friendly."

"Pretty nice truck he has."

"Yeah, brand new." Carlson's face lit up. "He ordered it. Has all the bells and whistles. Even has a dump truck horn."

"Didn't know that. How come you don't have a new truck?"

"Oh, I'll get one. Not like Moore's. I don't need anything that big. But I'm buying a boat first. I fish. Got it on order." Nodded his head with a huge smile at the idea and Cav let him talk brightly about the vessel's features.

"How come you took his truck this morning?"

"Donny said we had to take two cars. Mine's a clunker. Generally, runs real good. But it broke down this morning, and we had to drive Moore's truck. He wasn't happy about it. Carlson stopped and put his hand in front of his mouth.

"That's okay. We know Moore drove his truck."

"Oh, good, well then."

"So you and Moore just decided to go rob Payday?"

"Um. I don't want to talk about that."

"Okay. Tell me about Donny."

Carlson's eyes got huge. "No, I never said that." He waved his hand back and forth. "I don't know any Donny."

"Are you telling me this was your idea to rob the store?"

He shook his head violently. "No."

"Moore's?"

Carlson put his tongue between his pursed lips.

Cav waited, and then spoke gently. "Let me summarize. You have been arrested for attempted armed robbery, a felony which has a penalty up to fifteen years. You will be convicted, because I will testify as to what I saw." He let that sink in and said, "The D.A. might cut a deal with first offenders who help law enforcement. All that changes if there is any shooting."

Carlson looked down at his hands, stopped tapping and rubbed them together. Stopped. Looked up at the four men. "I want a deal."

"Tell us what we want to know; we'll speak to the D.A. But you got to tell all of it. Answer all our questions."

Carlson thought about it, finally nodded his head.

Cav didn't want to ask but did. "Do you want an attorney?"

"No."

Cav let out his breath. "Okay, who set up the robbery today?"

"Donny," Carlson said in a whisper.

"Who?"

"Donny. Donny Edwards. Him and that prick Evan Samples. It was all their idea."

"Why did Donny want two cars?"

"Cause he wanted to hit both shops at the same time," he complained. "We coulda done it with one car, but oh no, Mr. prick wanted two this time. They talked us into it. Made it sound so easy."

"This time?"

"Damn. I meant today, ya know."

Cav shook his head sadly. "That won't get you a deal. We know he and Samples hit Quick Check while you were in Payday. They are both in cells down the hall. In serious trouble."

"You got them, too? Did they shoot someone? Someone got killed? Is that what you were talking about?"

"No, Jack. I promised not to talk about any shooting without your attorney. I told you that. So, it was Donny's plan to hit both shops at the same time?"

Carlson nodded, keeping his head down.

"Jack, you have to say it."

"Donny planned it. Him and Samples. They said if we hit both shops, we'd have enough money to retire."

"Retire?"

"You know, not rob any more stores. I wanted to stop. They wouldn't let me," he whined.

"That wasn't fair. What car did they use?"

"Donny has this old little thing. Could barely fit the four of us."

"We didn't find a car registered in his name. Did you steal the car?"

Carlson shook his head. "Donny didn't steal it. He sorta borrowed it. From an old lady in the hospital. Dying. He said no one would notice it was missing. He bragged on it whenever we were together."

"You know who that lady is?"

"Nah. But her house is next door to Donny's aunt's house. Where he's living now? The aunt is taking care of the old lady's house. Donny's helping her. He even got our boss to pay him rent for the house. Mr. Newton needed a nice place for his buyers. There's some kinda glitch at the permitting department and he needed a place for these people. Donny had the keys and everything."

"So, Donny rented the old lady's house to your boss and used her car?" Cav encouraged him.

"Yeah. He's pretty smart with finance, you know. One of them guru guys."

"Ah ha. And you all squeezed into this small car for an earlier robbery?"

Carlson's eyes went back and forth between the detectives. He licked his lips again.

"We know about them, Jack," Cav said soothingly.

"You do?" he asked hopefully.

"Yep. But I need you to tell us. Where and when."

"I don't know if I can remember them all, the places I mean. I didn't pay much attention. Just kinda went along, you know?"

"Would it help if you could write them down, make a list? The best you can remember?"

"Yeah. That would help."

Cav handed over a yellow tablet and a pen. "When you finish the list, you can write out the whole story, okay?"

Carlson grabbed the pen and started writing and Cav said, "Detective Coleman is going to stay with you, wait for you to finish. If you need anything, just let him know."

Cav, Jones, and Chavez left. "We work our way up the food chain. Moore next. I want to know how this guy Samples fits in. If I'm not wrong, he's the mastermind. So change of plans, we save him for last.

Moore's attorney wanted a deal, but Cav shook his head. "Carlson is writing out a statement. He'll get the deal. Unless you have something really good. Something new. If so, we'll talk to the DA." Cav wasn't surprised to find Moore a whole lot less naïve. He sneered at Cav, "You can't con me. I suppose you want me to give you all the details. I wasn't born yesterday. Not saying nothing."

"We don't want details. Carlson gave us all of it. And we saw it ourselves. You forget we interrupted you while you were committing an armed robbery?"

Moore started to speak but his attorney put his hand on his arm. "What do you want?" he asked Cav.

"He could agree to testify against Carlson."

Moore sneered.

"And Samples and Donny."

Moore's head jerked up. "He gave you them?"

"Told you he gave us everything."

The attorney kept his hand on Moore's arm. "So, you what? Want more on those other men?"

"Yeah. You two need a minute?"

The attorney whispered in Moore's ear. Moore shook his head. The attorney continued whispering, got an angry nod.

"He'll give you what he knows on those two men. We want his sentence cut."

"Give us something we don't know, doesn't have to be about the robberies, and it's a deal."

The attorney nudged Moore. He gave them pretty much the same story they got from Moore.

"Donny stole that car he was driving. He tell you that?" Moore asked.

"We sort of heard that. Didn't believe it."

"Yeah. He stole it from his neighbor. Bragged about it. Drove around in it like it was some kinda Vette or Shelby. Thing couldn't go over forty-five. Was too small to hold a grown man. Who would brag about something like that? Only Dumb Shit Donny."

"Well that's interesting. The neighbor didn't notice Donny was driving his car?"

"Her? The neighbor's an old woman. She's in some kind of hospital, dying. Doesn't know he's got her car. He's renting her house, too. To our boss. For his customers."

"Your boss is renting the house?"

"Well, um, the boss is having trouble with his occupancy permit for the house he built for those clients, and he had to put them someplace. So, Donny rented the old lady's house."

"Sounds like a pretty smart guy to me. Has a free car, making money renting someone else's place. And he planned that heist."

"Wasn't him. It was that bastard Samples. He decides which check cashing shops to rob and when."

His attorney put his hand on his arm and he stopped talking.

"This something new for you?"

"Donny gave us Samples. He didn't like him either."

"He took forty percent of the take. Cause he planned it all.

Wasn't Donny. Too stupid. Samples planned it all. Look where we are today."

He didn't have anything further.

Donny was next. Cav was looking forward to it. The attorney wanted a deal on the table before he'd let Donny answer questions. So what else was new? Cav didn't even sit. "Carlson and Moore rolled on you and Samples. When we told Samples that, Samples not being his real name, he put it all on you. Just came in to let you know. Don't need your attorney after all, because we have nothing to discuss."

Donny cursed all three of his accomplices, the cops, his attorney. "If I hadn't waited for you," he told the attorney. "It's all your fault." He turned to Cav. "It was Samples. It was all his idea. His plan. Foolproof he said. No one would ever catch us." Donny shook his head and brushed his attorney aside. "Shut up. All I had to do was find a car and I did that. Found a car just like he said. It was all his idea. I just followed orders."

"What car?" Cav asked innocently.

"Stupid old bat next door. Her car. Some cheap compact. Subcompact. I wouldn't own a car like that. I got her car."

"Borrowed it?"

"Yeah. Borrowed it." He smirked.

"Carlson said you were really smart in finances. Got the car free. Rented that house."

"Yeah," Donny bragged. Snorted. "Didn't have to do nothing. Just told my boss I knew a place where he could put his buyers up, but they'd have to do the upkeep. He jumped on it. I was doing the old lady a favor. Got my great-aunt off my back. My idea."

"Samples suggest that?"

"What? No. That was all my idea." The attorney tried again to stop Donny, but he shook him off. "Samples don't know anything about that. But he did all the planning on the robberies. All of it. We just went along. Did what he told us."

"How did Samples know which shops to hit? When?"

"I don't know. He just did." Donny shrugged a shoulder. "He'd just give me a call and say, 'Friday, pick me up at nine' then tell me where to drive."

"You share the money equally?"

Donny shook his head. Stopped. "No. He divided out the money. He counted it out. Took most of it for his share. He deserved it, he said, 'cause he did all the planning."

"That hardly seems fair."

"See that proves he planned everything. He got the most money. Ask him about that, why don't you."

Jones stood. "Think I'll do that," he said and left the room after giving Cav a meaningful glance.

Cav sat back, kicked the breeze. "You're a pretty smart guy. Renting out that house for the old lady. You get a percentage of that rent? After all, you did all the work. Found the guy and everything."

"All my idea. Why would I share with that old biddy? She's lying in a bed waiting ta die. Doesn't even know what's going on."

"What about your aunt?"

"She don't know nothing. Another brainless old biddy. I done it. My idea. I mean the keys are sitting on that hook in the kitchen. The house is empty; my boss needs a place." He put his hands up.

"How much rent you charge, Donny? What's a place like that go for? What is it three, four-bedroom, two bath?"

"How'd I know? Needed the cash. Told him what I needed. He paid it."

Made sense, sort of. "How do you know Samples?" Cav already knew, wanted to know if Donny would tell the truth.

"We both got caught after that fire at the strip mall. Cops said we were looting."

"You weren't together?"

"Na. There were lots of guys helping themselves. Why not?" he said. "It was all kind of smoky. Anyhow the cops arrested a whole bunch of guys."

Cav leaned toward. "Well, Donny, if what you say is true, we may be able to cut some time off your sentence. You have any of the cash? We can get a search warrant, but it would be easier if you tell us where you hid it."

This time Donny did check with his attorney. Cav smiled to himself. They already had the warrant. He waited.

"It's in the car."

Cav showed his surprise.

"My aunt is always in my stuff. Cleaning and washing. Ain't got nothing private."

"Oh, okay. We'll be sure to get you a receipt. How much is left?"

Donny scowled. "Most of it. Well, almost most of it. Samples said he'd kill me if I started flashing it around." Then Donny smiled. "Shows how smart he is, don't it? Got half of it spent and he never noticed. Only thing was, I had to keep working construction or he'd have figured it out."

Donny got his own notepad to write down which shops they hit and when.

Cav and Chavez discussed their approach to Samples, but that turned out to be a waste of time. Samples wasn't talking and all the attorney would discuss were the charges and Samples's arraignment.

"They are all going down. Samples too. Especially since Carlson added those two liquor store holdups to his list. Salesclerk got hurt. That will add time to their sentences. Doesn't matter how good his attorney is," Cav remarked. "Where's Jones?"

"Going over Carlson's confession," Chavez replied.

Cav led him back to his office, passing Sally and smiling, because she was back to her normal self, insulting her fellow cops. It gave him an idea and he called her over. "Go in. Sit with Donny. I want to know how Samples knew what shops to hit. And when. Maybe suggest he's stupid. Can you do it?"

"Sure can." She hurried off.

Jones and Coleman caught up with them. "Got it all. Being typed up," Jones said.

"Good. Let's watch Sally." They all stood behind the one-way glass and watched the two people sit opposite each other saying nothing. It didn't take long. Donny began to fidget. Finally said," What are you doing in here?"

"Nothing. Just watching. Boss said to sit here with you while he talks to the brains of the outfit."

"Whadoyamean?"

Sally smiled. "Boss says Samples is the man to talk to. Samples is the brains of the outfit, hunh? I mean he knew what shops to hit and all. Guess that means you're the flunky."

Donny snorted. "He hit shops on paydays. No brains. Hit or miss. We were fine until the brains decides we don't have to go so far away. Should hit these two in town. Shoulda stayed in New York like I told him. Where there's more money. But, oh no, the moron says, hit these two. And look where we are. How's that for brains?"

And there it was. No inside man. Paydays were generally Thursday or Friday and that's when the shops, any shop, would have the most cash on hand. Pick a shop near a large business, wait for payday. No planning needed.

Cav waited for the men to be seated and said, "Okay. Chavez, compare statements. We'll talk with the aunt and the contractor. Sounds like they are both in the clear but check all the boxes."

He got a nod and continued. "FBI and DEA will be working the farmhouse and Estates case."

"Damn. They're moving in, taking over," Chavez interrupted.

"No. They're working with us. Taking over the parts we don't have the manpower or equipment for. Or the expertise. We're not trained to take down a fentanyl lab. We need them."

"We work with them?"

"Right. And run part of the operation. I have a meeting with them in—" he checked his watch, time was going quick—"forty minutes. Jones will be coming with me since he has been in on the case since the beginning and is our contact man." Cav didn't want any hurt feelings.

"You should take a detective with you," Coleman said.

Cav was surprised to find he was right about noses getting out of joint. And disappointed.

"I'm not saying don't take Jones, he's the best choice. He's been on the case from the beginning, like you said. I'm saying you'd look more commanding if he were a detective."

Cav's glare made him squirm in his seat. But he continued. "Damn it Boss, just promote the kid. Lord knows he deserves it. And he's making me look bad when I have to go to a uniform for help with a case. Pull him off traffic duty. It's embarrassing. Kid's got good instincts. Can see through the clutter. It would be better to have him as a permanent part of the detective force where we can utilize his ability. You got that opening. Put him in it. Kid is a natural."

First Chavez, now Coleman. Was he the only one who thought it would look like favoritism if he promoted Jones? Jones had taken the test and was at the top of the list.

He'd have to think on it. If he ever got a free moment.

On the way to the DEA meeting, Jones updated him on the Blake property which Stone had told them about "It was a meth lab. I talked with the cops, first on scene, and the fire inspector. It was arson."

Cav rolled that around in his brain for a while then concentrated on how he would work with the Feds.

DEA Agent Dawson was running the joint task force and would coordinate the raids. He gave a quick summary of the operation using maps and schematics, which he put on the white boards one by one beginning with the Estates house. Arrows pointed from it to the dealer tag numbers Cav's people had recorded with even more arrows pointing to more drug houses. Dawson had men working with local law enforcement at each location, surveilling the buildings, recording sales, and tracking both buyers and sellers.

It was impressive for, what was it, two days? Twelve sites, five states. Multiple vehicles and suspects. It all started with Lori, who was identified only as a confidential informant.

The farm, Kingstone's property, had its own whiteboard. No arrows to or from it.

"Sheriff," Dawson said when he was finished with the summary, "I know you want to close down your fentanyl factory immediately. Jones made a convincing argument. We tend to agree. But we'd like to leave it running. It's the first lead we've had into the new drugs flooding the area. We believe your farmhouse is the source. We want to wait for them to get a delivery of the drugs, so we can backtrack them. Also track anything leaving the farm. And we're hoping Eggert shows up. I promise none of the drugs will get out on the street."

Cav didn't have to go along with the Feds. He could raid the farm himself. The Feds didn't have to ask for his cooperation; they could demand it. But Dawson seemed to be saying, Cav's town, Cav's decision.

"You guarantee no drugs make it to the street?"

"Yes. I can do that. We don't want them out there any more than you do. We like your plan to stop the buyers at the Estates on traffic warrants. No one should spot the connection."

"How are you going to surveil the farm?"

"Heard you had some ideas on that," Dawson said.

Cav looked at Gibbs. "We have put that nice RV out there with a nice couple inside."

But the DEA agent shook his head. "We need electronics for surveillance."

"Don't need your stuff. The electronics in RV SPY are state of the art. I don't even have to see yours to know that," Cav said.

"RV spy? You named it?"

Cav smiled. "My man did. Kevin. We've used it before on stake-outs. He let us have it. Only problem is, we had to include Kevin with the RV. This vehicle has everything you could imagine, and more. Ask Gibbs."

"It has electronics? Not interested in Facebook and Pinterest. Will our stuff fit?" Dawson looked to Gibbs for more information, apparently trusting his opinion over Cav's.

"State of the art listening post. And Kevin is a good man—and knows how the equipment works. He installed it. Designed some of it. Can add anything you want. And he can keep his mouth shut."

Cav said, "We stuck a sold sign in that driveway a quarter mile north on the road and parked the RV there. It all looks normal. Plush RV, two young people, new home. It will work."

Dawson nodded. "Took a ride by. Where did you get the young couple?"

"Kevin and Becca Travis, ex-cop."

"Becca Travis. That name sounds familiar." Dawson looked at the ceiling. "Caught some big serial killer recently?"

Cav snorted. "More than one and besides, she's married to Gibbs here."

Dawson looked at Gibbs again. Nodded slowly. "Okay. Since they're already in place, we don't want to change things up. Couple of my people will join them."

Things were moving in the right direction. DEA and FBI would work the drug operation, He was relieved the Feds were taking over. He didn't have the manpower to surveil both locations, twenty-four hours a day, let alone follow the vehicles coming and going.

His cell rang as he and Jones headed for his car. Lori.

"Hey, honey."

"Oh, yeah. Hi," she said. "Um. My really cute brother and my hot boyfriend are both invited to the final shuffleboard tournament playoff at Forest this evening. Starts in about two hours. To be followed by a celebration buffet and gala."

"Aw gee, I don't know honey."

"This will be your chance to meet the residents, some family members and friends, and most of the staff. Give you a chance to see how the place works and if anyone looks suspicious."

She had a point. He checked his watch. "We have a stop to make first. Two stops. Might be late, but we'll be there."

He told Jones and smiled when Jones frowned and said, "Whoopee. Seriously? We're going to a shuffleboard game?"

"Yeah. My sentiments too."

"Ha. You don't need me for that."

Cav smiled. "I gotta go to shuffleboard. You gotta go to shuffleboard. We'll get a chance to observe interactions. Get a free meal. Maybe learn how this drug mob finds vacant homes. But first we have interviews."

They'd caught the check cashing thieves and the guy mugging the homeless. Now they would concentrate on the occupied properties and interview the contractor, Jeffrey Newton, about the blue house and John Steward about Stone's farm. "We'll talk with Steward, he's three blocks away and then see Newton, the contractor." Steward looked honest on paper, and Kevin said he had a good reputation. But there was only one way to find out and they had a cover story.

Home Stewards occupied a storefront in a strip mall between a dollar store and a dentist. They walked into an open area with a counter across the back. "Help you?" a clerk asked.

"Looking for Steward," Cav said, showing his badge.

The clerk's eyes went big. "Wow. Um, sure." He turned and

hollered through a door leading to the back. "Hey, Stew, some cops here to see you."

"Gave last week when they came by," a voice said.

"Not collecting, Mr. Steward. We have some questions concerning a couple of addresses you are managing."

"Problem at one of them?" He came to the doorway. "Break-in? When? Which one? What do you mean couple?"

"Can we go in your office and talk? Maybe check the addresses?"

"Sure. Sure. Come on back." He led them to a tiny office. Bookcases and file cabinets lined the walls. Three whiteboards. Two listed addresses, owner name, employee name, days for service for the week. The third seemed to be monthly.

Cav didn't see Stone's name.

"That's our visits for each week," Steward said motioning to two of the boards. "The other is our monthly. Which properties?"

Cav pulled out his notebook, made up a name. "Neena Kolberg. Don't see her on your boards."

But Steward was already shaking his head. "Nope. Not a client. Whew. All our clients are on the boards. Only thing we change is the dates. Add or subtract new customers, of course."

"You don't have to check your files?"

"Not if she's a current of recent client. I know them all." But he bent over and opened a file drawer. Pulled out a file. "Have a list here. We keep it updated." He ran a finger down the page. Then down another.

"Nope. Not here. You said a couple of customers?"

"Ian McNight?" Kevin had given him that name. One of his clients who had hired Stewards.

"He's here. We worked for him for three months. He sold his property six months ago. That it? What's this about?"

"Can you check your files for a Mr. Kingstone?" Cav read off the address.

"Remember that one. Seemed like a nice guy. Plush job for us, even if it was way out in the middle of nowhere. Shame about the guy."

"What do you mean?"

"Well he died. Something like that sticks with you, you know?"

"Died?"

"Yeah. About three months ago. Here, I'll get you our notification."

He pulled open a bottom file drawer in one of the cabinets and rifled through the files. Pulled one out. "We were kind of hoping the attorney would keep us on, but…" He looked at a paper in the file. "Right, they let us go with a thank you. We wrote back about money paid in advance and didn't they want to keep us on, never heard back. Guess I dropped the ball on that." He handed over the file.

Cav thumbed through it, handed it to Jones, gave Steward the other address. "Don't remember this one." He found another file, looked inside. Nodded his head. "Okay. This is more typical. Property sold. New owner didn't need our services." He gave Cav the file back.

"We'd like copies, if we could, and I'd appreciate if you kept our conversation to yourself."

"Sure. Sure. Just glad it wasn't one of our current properties. Black mark if that happened, you know."

"They're clear," Cav said on the way back to the car. "And you cleared the other property managers. It's someone in the hospital. Because it looks like a couple of the properties were being used before the owners moved into Forest. Or is Forest notified a day or two ahead to expect a new resident? Their snoop tells them a homeowner dies or moves into Forest and won't be going home. They set up, but suddenly they discover the owner is moving back. They resort to arson to destroy what they can't move out in time. Makes sense they would add someone at Forest. Someone who knows when patients are scheduled to go home. Who has come into a lot of money recently? Someone with access to incoming mail, maybe? Or, and I lean toward this one, the property owners told the hijackers themselves. The same way they told Max. Have our people follow up on those attorney letters, but they're probably fake."

Seemed like every step forward opened a dozen more questions to track down and answer.

Jones took notes.

They found Newton at the house where the puddle jumper had been parked. The same man Jones had talked to earlier met them at the door. "Hey. You get hired?" he asked with a smile. "Boss didn't say anything."

"Need to see him. Is he here?"

"Trailer. Out back. Using it for an office." He nodded to the left. "Go through there."

They followed his directions down a hall not yet drywalled and out a back door. Black steel. Temporary by the looks of it. The trailer was five steps across a dirt yard. They knocked and entered when a voice said, "Come in."

"Mr. Newton?" Cav asked.

"Right. What can I do for you folks? Got to tell you upfront, not hiring." He came around his desk which was a sheet of plywood on two sawhorses covered with blueprints and Cav could see what looked like a daily schedule.

Cav laughed. "We're not looking for work. I'm Sheriff Cavanaugh." He pointed at Jones. "My deputy, Jones." Both Cav and Jones showed ID.

"This about my boys?" Newton asked, disgusted. "Word got around pretty quick they got caught during an armed robbery." He shook his head.

"Three of your employees," Cav said.

"Idiots." Newton motioned to two rickety folding chairs. "Sit. Sit." He went behind his desk. "Dumb jerks. Don't know what I can tell you. Didn't expect that from Donny or Carlson, either one of them. Wouldn't think either of them have the brains to set up a robbery. Or the guts to follow through. Tempted to say Carlson goes wherever he's led."

"Hmm," Cav said noncommittally. Might as well get some questions answered. "What about Moore?"

"Him? Yeah, him I can see. Smarter than the other two put together, though that's not saying much."

"What kind of work did they do?"

"Donny does sheetrock, when he works. Carlson too, and tiles. Good and quick. Gives me an eight-hour day. Donny, not so much. Moore's day labor, go for, helper, clean-up. No skills."

"Why hire Donny?" Cav asked.

"I needed an extra man and he came looking. He knows how I work, and I don't have to waste time training a new guy. We have a deal. I give him a small advance, and I pay him when the job is done. Otherwise he disappears after his first paycheck."

"He and Carlson buddies on the job?"

"About the same as everyone. We get along here. Don't know about after work."

Cav nodded; the information backed up what they already knew. "Actually, we're here about the house you rented from Donny."

He slapped himself lightly on the forehead. "Damn. No. Don't tell me there's something kinky with that. There's no way Donny was pulling a fast one. I even talked to his great aunt, the lady next door. Donny's helping her rent it."

"How did that work? What did she say?"

"Well, now you mention it, Donny did all the talking. Only spoke with the aunt once. What he told me was the lady who owns the property asked them to look after it. Rent it, Donny said, while she's traveling. Just have to make sure we leave her stuff alone, clean up when we move out. I gave him a check for a full three weeks on the spot. Fair rate."

"Who did you make the check out to?"

"The aunt. I can look it up for you."

"Appreciate that."

Newton picked up a blueprint on the corner of his desk and pulled out a business checkbook. Opened it and paged back. "Had a problem with the occupancy permit on the four-bedroom home I built them. Frustrating. House is sitting there empty and waiting and the county is fixing a computer glitch. I'm not the only builder waiting. 'Soon.' they keep saying." He stopped, flipped more pages. "Here it is, Mrs. Weldon. That's the aunt. Donny gave me the keys." He passed the book over and continued. "Nice family in there. Easy to work with. Knew what they wanted in a home. Not happy to be renting, but it's a nice place. I call every day after I talk to the county. Go see them every three or four days. Please don't tell me there's something wrong."

"Can you make a copy for us? Of the check?"

"Check's not back yet, but sure—when it comes."

"Maybe we can get copies of Donny's timesheets. And Carlson's, Moore's?" Another lock, Cav thought.

Newton had a small copier-printer on a two-drawer file cabinet and turned to make the copy. "Give me an e-mail and I'll send them electronically."

Jones handed a card over. "Appreciate it."

Cav asked, "What about the car?"

"What car?" Newton responded, distracted.

"The one Donny kept parked here."

"Oh, yeah. Forgot about that. Said the old lady didn't want the car on the street. Didn't make much sense, but I got plenty of space here. Sort of seemed like a condition for the rental." He rubbed his head. Pulled his hair. Cav recognized the tell. "What's wrong with the car?" He closed his eyes. "Wait. I didn't notice it there today. Don't tell me it's been stolen."

"Not from your lot. Thanks for your help." Cav stood, held out a hand. Shook. "We'll be looking for your email."

"Get it off right now."

They went back out the way they came in, thanking the foreman.

"Not him," Jones said.

"No. He never really was in the running. But we had to eliminate him. The blue house was different. Not connected to what's happening at Forest."

"You like that blue house?" Jones asked.

"Oh yeah. Always have," Cav said a little wistfully. "Something about it touches me." He felt silly when he heard himself say that. Grimaced. Pulled his hair and before he could modify it, Jones said, "Lori too. When we were little and came home from school, she always picked the route past that house. Would drag her hand across the picket fence and say, 'Someday this is going to be my house.'"

Cav hadn't known that. Something else to think about. She loved the house he loved. He loved her. He almost asked Jones what Lori wasn't telling him but stopped just in time before embarrassing himself further. He hadn't worked up the guts to tell Jones he was going to marry Lori.

By the time they arrived at Forest, people were gathered in the common room which was festive with green banners hanging from the ceiling. Pink and green tissue paper and balloons were strung from the bright chandeliers. Posters of the finalists decorated the walls.

Lori introduced them to the managers. "Benjamin Roberts, my brother Andy and a friend." Her friend or her brother's friend, she left ambiguous.

"Ben, call me Ben," he said shaking hands.

"And John," Lori continued. "His second in command."

Benjamin, Ben, was a short fat cheerful guy. Bald. John the opposite. Tall, Cav had to look up to him, solid, with a mane of long dark hair. Bet he's called Little John, Cav thought. Or Mutt. No. Jeff was the tall one.

When Cav asked if they would be playing outside on a lighted court, they looked at him in puzzlement and then Ben laughed. "Oh, no. We play inside."

"You have an indoor court?"

"No. This is table shuffleboard."

"You don't play it outdoors on a big green court with a chalked diamond with numbered triangles at each end? Using those long cue sticks?" Cav asked surprised.

"No. No, no. This is table shuffleboard. Over there by the far wall." He pointed to where people were gathered and cheering. "Of course, we have outdoor courts also. But this indoor tournament is one of our highlights. We always follow it with a buffet dinner." He pointed in the opposite direction to long tables ready for food.

"The kids are a little rambunctious tonight," Ben said

"Kids?" Cav asked, puzzled again. He didn't see any children.

"Residents. I call them my kids. They act very much like five-year olds. Very big five-year olds. Which wouldn't be so bad if they didn't have about sixty or seventy years of experience getting into mischief. They are sometimes a handful, right Lori?"

"Lori is one of our best independent contractors," John said.

"Best," Ben corrected. And Cav could hear the respect in his tone. "Have you made a decision, my dear?"

Cav raised an eyebrow. "Decision?"

"Yes. She—"

But Lori interrupted taking his hand. "Let's go talk. Cav? You and Andy wander over and look at the shuffleboard table, I'll catch up."

She led Ben off.

He watched her walk away. A decision. One that had to do with Ben. And Forest? One she couldn't share with him? He shrugged and followed Jones to join the crowd around a long narrow waist high table about fourteen feet long with numbered bands on either end. The wooden surface looked slick. One player sprinkled very fine sand beads on it.

"Why is he putting sand on the table?" Jones asked.

"We wax the surface before a game. The sand decreases the friction between the table and the puck. Increases the speed." When Jones laughed at the terminology, calling sand "wax," the guy showed him the container. It clearly called the sand a wax. Hmph. Jones had a lot to learn about the game.

The goal of table shuffleboard, like the one played on the court, was to get the highest score. A player stood at one end of the table and slid a puck to the other end. Each team of two people chose a color, red or blue. Cav shook his head because the team was split up, one player on opposite sides of the table.

Each team here at Forest was identified by some sort of crazy hat or head gear. The men in the wide brimmed green straw hats were leading. The two ladies wearing the bright blue wigs were close behind. He saw a hat trimmed in pink roses with two pink flamingoes on top, one with huge elephant ears, a giant Spam can, another with blinking lights. He was a little surprised not to see the college beer can cap, but then he realized these folks were probably past that stage. He didn't see any liquor at all. And Ben was right; the residents were high without it.

While they watched, one guy slid a blue puck toward the opposite end of the table. His competitor shot the red. They alternated shots aiming for the end of the table and the high score band. Or better yet, apparently, one player would knock his opponent's puck off the table into the alley. When each had shot all their pucks, the highest score was entered into the table's electronic board which tallied the scores. Then their partners shot from the opposite end of the table. Cav watched, somewhat fascinated.

Each shooter leaned down over his weighted puck, placed his hand on it or around it, carefully judged distance, and pushed or 'shot' his puck down the 'waxed' table. Some held the puck between thumb and forefinger. Others rested two or three fingers on the top. One guy leaned way over and raised his leg like he was bowling.

The game didn't require power, strength, or endurance. The fans were having more fun than the players. They oohed and ahhed whenever a player made a good 'pitch', groaned when the shot was bad or fell off the board into the gutter. They didn't seem to be rooting for anyone in particular and called out encouragement or sympathy indiscriminately.

Cav alternated his attention between the table, the kids, and the buffet. Staff was busy bringing out food and it wasn't all fruits and vegetables. He spotted two crock pots with meatballs, one with a tomato sauce, the other a white sauce. He decided he'd try both. Maybe he could sneak some during the game when no one was looking. He'd get the roast beef chunks first, maybe over some rice with gravy. And the chocolate chip brownies. Nope. The strawberry cream cookie they just put out. Both.

An old lady pushed over to stand beside him, clearing her way with her cane, narrowly missing Jones head. "I'm Lucinda," she said. "Two B. Diagonally across the hall from Max. Saw you go in there yesterday." She nodded her head sagely. "Saw that cute guy go in with you. Don't see him tonight. I saw Stone go in."

The woman must live with her eye on the peephole.

"He's dancing with Max, doncha know. Stone is. So don't get your hopes up."

Dancing?

"That really cute man with you tonight, Lori's brother? Like that girl. Good at her job. Yep." She nodded her head. "Is her brother dancing with anyone? He could dance with me."

Dance?

She nodded again. "Yep. He could." She motioned to her right with her cane. "That guy over there in the elephant hat. Gordon.

Wouldn't mind dancing with him. But he's dancing with Mary, in the suit over there."

In the suit, right, Cav thought. Red jogging suit with rhinestones, wearing a neon blue wig. Eighty if she was a day. Huh? Elephants, dancing?

"That's a cute hat he has on. I wonder how they did the ears. Don't eat the carrots at the buffet. You'll recognize them—they look like beets. Taste like them too. Horrible."

Carrots? He looked at the buffet. He decided right then he'd try the meatballs in the white sauce. He'd start there. No carrots or beets though. Wasn't eating either of those.

But she was poking him in the ribs with the cane handle. Nodding to a young man beside the guy in the elephant hat. Muscled. Dark hair. "He's Gordon's grandson, Gordon the third. We call him The Third," she confided. "Comes twice a week to visit Gordon. He has an eye on one of the staff, Casey."

Lucinda nodded toward another young woman, in her early thirties, Cav guessed. "Cindy. She's dancing with Reggie, the redhead beside her. Nice young man. Management you know. Both of them. Always very pleasant. They speak with me every day, ask how I am. Want to know when I'll sell my house."

Cav's ears perked up at that. But Lucinda was busy pointing out a sad dumpy woman in dull purple. One who was staring at Jones, angrily. "That senior citizen behind her? She's Grumpy. Living proof 'you can't go home'. Her grandniece is a nice young woman. Brought me my shawl once when I was chilled. Comes every Saturday for lunch. She was really burned up when Grumpy said the doctor wanted her to go home. Grumpy wasn't too happy about it, said the doctor insisted. As if. Doctors don't do that."

Four people, two in flowered straw hats, two with plain silver tray hats cheered loudly. "Losers," Lucinda said tapping her cane on his foot. "They got knocked out already. Not much good. They don't care, they have more fun joking with the crowd."

Lucinda cackled. "Ohh, she was angry."

Who was angry?

"Yeah, burned up. Or is that down? Hah. Can't move now, of course. Almost feel sorry for her. Unpronounceable name. Both of them."

Both? Who? The straw hats? No, Lucinda was looking at the woman in the purple dress.

"Grumpy and Dizzy. Izzy really, but Grumpy is always ordering her around 'til she gets frazzled and doesn't know what she's doing." Lucinda nodded her head at a young, comparatively, woman standing by the Frump.

"Yep. They come to all the games, doncha know. Watch. Never cheer. But Dizzy floats around, talks to us. Grumpy stands and frowns."

Cav didn't think the name Dizzy fit the grandniece. She seemed to have it together.

"Don't eat the bacon. It's almost always burned to a crisp. People here don't like to chew, doncha know. No teeth." She smiled at him with a full set of bright white dentures.

Before Cav could respond, she poked him and pointed. "Never seen two hangers in a game before."

Hangers? He looked where she was pointing. Two pucks half off the edge of the shuffleboard. She turned her clouded blue eyes up to him and explained. "A hanger is when the puck hangs over the edge. You get an extra point for that. And they'll measure those to see which one will count. The blue one is Alice's." Lucinda pointed to the lady whose hat was pink roses and flamingoes. "Joan's is the red puck. She's wearing the Spam can hat. Pretty dumb hat if you ask me. Her too, for that matter. Has her eye on Gordon, but he doesn't see her."

She raised her cane again, this time aiming for Cav's nose. He moved back. "Today, I graduated to this cane. Yesterday I was on a walker. It had a seat so I could sit when I got tired."

She tilted her head. "Saw you with Big Honcho and Little John. We let them think they run the place. But Big H. and Little J. work for us." Ben and John, Cav decided, since he had thought Little John too, when he'd been introduced.

"Is he dancing with anyone?" he was curious, now.

"Oh my no." She thought a minute. "Well maybe with his wife. But I wouldn't know anything about that. Or anything about Little J." She looked around absently.

"That woman in the pink sweater? Management too. Nasty piece of work. Won't give any of us the time of day. Not dancing with anyone, no surprise."

"What's her name?"

"Nasty. But you could call her Shara."

She nodded to herself. "Nice to have young people around. We really need some of that diversity they're always talking about on the TV. Not enough men here. And no young people. Only old people live here. That man in the plaid shirt? He doesn't talk about his dancing partner, but," she raised a finger in the air, "I'll find out. I have my ways." She turned slightly to the left, "That's Annette in the pretty blouse."

He looked over. Pretty? The blouse was a blinding Hawaiian print shirt in hot yellow with red sharks and lime green palm trees.

"Annette's—"

He never found out about the woman in the pretty shirt because Lori rescued him. "I need to borrow my man, Mrs. Oberman. Are you okay? This is your first day with the cane. You don't want to overdo. Want me to walk you to a chair?

"Why thank you dear. That's so sweet. I am tired, but I don't want to lose my place."

Lori nudged Cav.

"Oh," he said. "May I bring you a chair Mrs. Oberman?"

"That would be nice. Such a nice young man, Lori. Is he dancing with anyone?"

Cav brought her a chair. She sat and pointed with her cane. "Bring one for Larry too, please; he's too macho to ask for himself." Cav saw two other residents looking enviously at Lucinda and nudged Jones. Together they brought over twelve chairs. He didn't think they needed the chairs, just liked the idea of someone supplying them.

They were old, but not what he'd expect. Not helpless and drooling in wheelchairs. They were active and alert. Like Stone and Max. In fact, most looked like they could get their own chairs, if they'd wanted them. 'Kids' was right. Peanut gallery was all he could think. Peanut gallery with wrinkled faces. He smiled at the thought and looked hopefully at the buffet.

The game didn't last much longer. The elephant ears won. Elephant ears? He looked at the buffet. Wonder if there were any elephant ears. Probably not. Had to be fried or something didn't they? His mouth watered.

The winners won tickets for free meals for a month. Lori whispered in his ear. "They all get free meals. But the winners sit at the head table and are served first. They also have their picture taken and put on the winner wall."

Max and Stone came by and they headed for the buffet. The food was good, and he went for seconds. Residents and staff came by their table to greet Lori's guests, so Cav met most of the people attending. He wasn't sure how much he learned, but he hadn't gotten any bad vibes. A few things Lucinda said warranted further clarification. He could ask Lori.

# FRIDAY

Sally called as Cav and Jones compared impressions the next morning. "Jones said you wanted to know if we caught any complaints on abandoned properties. I can't get ahold of Jones; he's out on a secret mission."

Secret mission? Cav pulled his hair. It was almost funny. Jones spends time with the Feds and he's on a secret mission. "He's with me. What do you have, Sally?" As soon as he said it, he wondered if he should have called her by her last name, like he did all his male deputies. Was it harassment to call her by her first name? He'd have to ask Lori; she always offered solutions to his dilemmas. Then he remembered he called the new patrolman, Carl, by his first name.

"Got a woman here who just found her home vandalized. She's living at Forest. This is her first visit home in two months. Boss, this place has extensive damage, not just a mess but destroyed here. Not ordinary vandalism."

"You go inside?"

"No. I just looked in through the front door, walked around the building, looked in windows. I stayed clear of footprints, Boss. The owner didn't go in either; she just looked and collapsed on the stoop here. She's really torn up, might need more rehab after this." Sally rushed on with her report. "She's okay, sitting on the front stoop with her caregiver. Your, um, your, ah, um…"

His cell beeped. "Um, what?" he asked, not patiently, pulling his hair.

"Her, um, her therapist. Um," Sally slowed down and stopped.

"What Sally?' He tugged at a strand.

"Um. Her caregiver, therapist? It's Lori Jones. Um, Jones's sister. Um, your, um." She stopped again.

Great. He pulled his hair again. Hard this time. Sure. It would be Lori. Yup. Of course. And Sally called her my, um. Did everyone know?

"Ms. Jones told me to call you direct."

An incoming text from Lori. He read it quickly. Same info.

"Sit with Ms. Jones and the owner. Stay outside. Let no one in. We'll be there in ten. I'll send Chavez and EDU. I don't want anyone in that building until the Evidence Detection Unit works through the scene."

Jones drove. They found three squad cars in front of the house, which was an older, slightly rundown home on an older, slightly rundown residential street. A block from the seedy part of town— sex shops, strip clubs, adult bookstores, X-rated movies. Every city had seedy.

He walked over to Lori and ran a hand down her shoulder, nodded to the old lady on the stairs.

Lori waved a hand toward the entrance. "The door's off the hinges. And the stink." She wrinkled her nose. "The stink was horrible. I think that upsets her as much as the physical damage. We could see the inside was wrecked."

"Give me a minute." He stepped to the door where Sally and Chavez stood waiting. Peeked inside. It was a mess. And it did stink.

Sally said, "Door was half off the hinges when they got here. No one has been inside." She motioned to the woman on the doorstep. "Owner, Ida Rydel."

"Evidence Detection Unit goes in there first. Make's sure it's safe," Cav instructed.

Chavez pulled out his notebook. "I sent cops to knock on doors, canvass the neighbors. Sally and I'll talk to the people out on the sidewalk there."

Chavez called her Sally. Did that mean it was okay?

Cav took another look inside and turned back to the owner. Lori had her arm around the woman, rocking her. Cav watched a minute. That's what he loved about her. Care and comfort which came so naturally to her. She looked up at him with helpless eyes. Shook her head. "Why? Why would anyone do that?"

Because they could. Because they didn't care. He thought it, didn't say it. Same as he hadn't asked her about her 'decision'. He had hoped she would explain what Ben meant, but she hadn't. He stooped down in front of the woman, put a hand on her knee. "Mrs. Rydel, can you talk?"

She raised her tear-filled eyes toward him and nodded. Held onto Lori's hand.

"You live at Forest, right?"

"Yes."

"When did you move there?"

"About six weeks ago."

She looked to Lori who confirmed. "EMTs took her to the hospital two months ago." She patted Mrs. Rydel's hand.

Ida nodded. She put the Kleenex up to her eyes. "One of my neighbors called in a health and safety check when they didn't see me for two days. They found me on the floor unconscious. I stayed in the hospital for two weeks and then transferred to Forest for therapy and decided to stay."

"Can you tell me why you came today?"

Ida shook her head and Lori answered this time. "To pick up some personal things she wanted." She frowned and shook her head in anger.

"Was this visit scheduled?" he asked.

"No," Ida replied.

"So, you just decided today to come get some things?"

"Yes. I... I was supposed to come out three weeks ago, but I got sick."

Huh?

EDU arrived and put on masks and hazmat gear. The leader, Bruce, stopped to ask if anyone had entered the building and then joined his team and headed inside

A man slipped past the deputies and strode toward them. "Ida. Ida. Where have you been?"

Cav blocked his way. "Who are you sir?"

"I'm Joseph Porter. I live a few houses down and across the street."

Ida looked up at him with tears streaming down her cheeks. "Joey. I thought you would call. Or come and visit."

"Ida. I did call. All my calls went to voicemail and you never called back. And your voicemail is full."

"Oh. My phone. I think it broke when I fell. I was in the hospital and never thought of it. I kept meaning to replace it, but it just seemed to be too much effort."

He sat on her other side and hugged her. "We're going to get you a new phone and you're going to list me as ICE, 'in case of emergency'. I'll add you to mine."

"Hold it. Hold it. You folks can get reacquainted later. Let me ask the questions." In gentle tone Cav asked, "Mrs. Rydel, you were supposed to come out three weeks ago?"

"Yes. I decided I was ready to move back home. My doctor wasn't sure. But Lori, Lori thought we could come look and arranged it." She patted Lori's hand.

"But I had a relapse. Bad food? Something disagreed with me and I spent two days in bed. In my room," she added hastily, "not the hospital. I wasn't that sick." She wept into Joseph's shoulder, and he hugged her close.

Cav had a dismaying thought, shades of Lucinda. Were they dancing? If not, they probably would be soon.

"Where are you living?" Porter asked. "I couldn't find you. I couldn't find you. Where have you been? I searched for you."

"Didn't the hospital tell you where I was?"

"No. By the time I found the right hospital, you were gone, and they wouldn't tell me anything. And these other people moved in a week later."

"They trashed my house," Ida wailed and began crying again.

Cav led Porter a few steps away. "You called for the health and safety check?"

"Yeah. Didn't see her for two whole days and she didn't answer her door. EMT's took her away. Couldn't find her." He looked down.

"Tell me about the people who moved in here."

"They wouldn't talk to us. Unfriendly. Belligerent actually. Tough looking."

"Vehicles?"

"Well, different ones. Have some license plate numbers. I kept track. Car descriptions. At home in a notebook."

Cav looked up, hopeful. "That would help. I'll send one of my officers with you to get it."

Porter nodded. "Those people left about three weeks ago. Seemed in a hurry. And then the kids showed up."

EDU motioned they could go in. Bruce said, "No power. Be careful, we marked some weak spots in the floor."

Cav stooped by Lori. "A few more minutes."

Bruce handed him a flashlight. Chavez went for two more.

The damage was about what Cav expected. Furniture was a pile of broken rubble in a corner, rugs burned and stained. Holes punched in walls and graffiti spray painted on the remaining walls.

"Used the chair legs on the walls." Chavez swung his flashlight on a chair leg still stuck in a hole. The kitchen was worse. Doors pulled off cupboards and the contents pulled out, opened and emptied on the floor. Broken china and glassware which crunched underfoot. Bathrooms had toilets pulled from walls, sinks broken.

"Why do they do this?" Jones asked. "I mean they have a nice place, why destroy it? Why live in filth? What does it take to keep things decent? Why act like animals? Not even animals. Animals don't foul their own nest."

All good questions, Cav thought. He didn't have any answers. They did a complete walk through the house, but the crooks hadn't left any business cards. Even so, they learned something.

"These guys pulled out about three weeks ago," Chavez said looking at his notes. "About the same time the place in the Estates started operations. So, looks like they moved their base of operations for some reason." He looked around. "This spot is perfect, I would think. At least for locals. Even distribution for the out of town crews. Moved out for some reason and didn't burn the place down."

Cav nodded. "Mr. Porter there confirms your timeline. And, coincidently, Mrs. Rydel was supposed to come out three weeks ago. But conveniently took sick. Maybe the dealers figured another arson fire would be dangerous."

He went back to Mrs. Rydel. Her eyes red and swollen and still she tried to smile for him. "I thought I was going to move back home. But everyone was so nice to me when I was sick, I decided to stay at Forest." She did manage the smile, but it broke down into another round of sobbing.

"When did you decide that?"

"This week."

"I need to get her back," Lori said. "She needs to lie down."

"Okay," Cav said. Dancing?

"I know you," Mrs. Rydel said, really looking at him for the first time. "You're Lori's young man. I saw you last night. Who did this?"

"Kids maybe. That's what we're going to find out. Now Ms.

Jones is going to take you back to Forest, and Mr. Porter can meet you there. After he gets us those vehicle descriptions." He looked to Porter who took the hint and hurried off. Chavez went with him.

Mrs. Rydel looked up. "If I had come back? If I had, would I have saved my home?"

Cav stooped down in front of her. Took her free hand. Patted it. "No. Whoever was here, had been here for some time. Probably most of the time you were gone. Neither of you went in, right?"

"No," Lori said again.

Ida stammered, "Can you? Can you find my wedding pictures?"

"We can't take anything out of the house." He'd almost called it a crime scene. "Not until my men have, um, checked over everything." He gave Lori a meaningful glance and shook his head minutely. Doubted they'd find any photographs, but he'd tell his men to look. "We'll look for whoever did this."

"Can I take her back to Forest? She needs to get away from this," Lori asked again.

"Yes. Someone will be by to talk to her, both of you," he said.

"Find the kids who did this," Mrs. Rydel said.

But it wasn't kids. And it looked like the drug dealers not only knew Ida was incapacitated but knew she was due back three weeks ago. More evidence that the culprit was at Forest. Knew she'd be sick? Made her sick?

"Come on Chavez." Should he call him Thomas? The hell with it.

"You really think it was kids?" Chavez asked.

"No. Yes. Drug house was abandoned about three weeks ago after Ms. Rydel decided to come home. Then, I think, it became a party house for teenagers. Empty beer bottles. Used condoms. The firepits to make the place feel like the great outdoors. Yeah, kids. And we'll find their fingerprints. I saw some charge receipts mixed in the debris on the floor. We'll get them." With any luck they'd be able to get a name, a fast food shop. A shop could have cameras.

He looked around the people behind the tape. "Someone out there knows. Sally will find them."

Chavez nodded. They walked back to the car, sat. Jones joined them, standing beside the car while they waited for EDU to finish. Cav sat thinking, jerking at his hair. Grunted. "Screwed up."

"What? When?" Chavez asked.

"This one here? Today? Someone at Forest knew Mrs. Rydel was coming home three weeks ago. And the drug dealers knew she was coming. Someone at Forest warned them."

"Damn. I don't know, Boss," Jones said. "We ran all the employees. Just a few bumps. Same with managers. And I didn't see anything off last night at shuffleboard." He said the last with a grin and a shake of his head.

"Not an employee. It's a resident. Or a resident's relative or friend. Let's expand the search. Get a list of residents. Then we look at their relatives, people who visit. They have to sign in, right?"

"Supposedly, yeah, but I don't think everyone does. It's kind of an honor system."

Cav frowned. Looked at the car ceiling. Something at the edge of his mind. What had Lucinda said? Something about last names. It rang a bell. Apparently not a loud bell because it took overnight for him to hear it.

"What's Brouska's name?"

"Brouska," Jones said.

Cav gave him a look that made him cringe. "His name. What's his name? His real name, not our shorthand nickname version."

Jones tapped his tablet. "Hold on. I don't remember. No one can spell it, no one can pronounce it. Brouskovetski."

"Right. That's what Lucinda said last night. Unpronounceable last names."

"Lucinda?"

"The lady who almost got your family jewels."

"Almost got my eye too."

"Grumpy."

"Not grumpy. Just saying."

"No. She said Grumpy's house burned down. Grumpy whose last name is unpronounceable. Has a grandniece who went ballistic when Grumpy said staff was taking her home. The next day. And the next day her house burned down. We don't have that house in our database. It's the first one. The first arson. They burned the building to hide any evidence of drugs and dealers. Didn't want to incapacitate the owner—or couldn't—and there was not enough time to move everything out and clean-up. So, they burned the evidence. She's where they started. The old lady, Grumpy. What's her name?"

"Grumpy. I don't know."

"Lucinda calls her Grumpy. Because she blows hot and cold. Sometimes very friendly, other times won't even speak. Had on a purple dress last night. Grumpy has an unpronounceable last name. Brouska has an unpronounceable last name. Coincidence? And the grandniece. Comes every Saturday for lunch. Dizzy. Lucinda calls her Dizzy."

"You think Grumpy and Brouska are related? That's a wide jump boss."

Cav glowered at him.

"Even if he is, you think he burned down his own relative's house?" Jones asked unbelieving.

"Don't know the relationship. And yes, I think he did. Need to talk to our go-to guy."

He pulled out his cell, spoke into it, his eyes still on Jones. "Deputy. Cav. You're on speaker, Max. Grumpy. The woman Lucinda calls Grumpy. What's her name?"

"Oh, um, her name is Bettina. I'm not sure of her last name. Wait, I have it here in our list of residents." He heard paper rattling. "Um, let me spell it out; I can't pronounce it. No one here can." She spelled it out. "B-e-t-t-i-n-i-s-d-e-k."

Damn. Not Brouska. Could he be wrong? Watched Jones write it down.

"Bettina Bettinisdek," Max said. "Hah, I can pronounce it. Why do you want to know?"

He almost didn't tell her, but she was part of the team. "Before you arrived at Forest, maybe while Stone was in the hospital, her house burned down." Or was it up? Now Lucinda had him confused. "It's not in your database."

"I didn't know that. Huh. Guess it's a good thing I retired as an agent. Can't believe I missed an important fact like that. Didn't look back. Well, that's an excuse. Another is that no one talks about Betty. Still, I'm sorry. Forgot to look back."

He interrupted her. "I told you not to ask questions, remember? To let people talk to you. You were not digging for information. You did a good job."

"Oh. Oh, thank you. Want me to talk to Bettina?"

"No. Not yet." He disconnected. "Not Brouska. Damn." Thought some more. Jones watched him. "Check arsons," he told Jones and waited.

"Three fires around our time period. The first, seven months ago. Owner, Howard O'Reilly." He scrolled down. The next, a very long unpronounceable name. Bettinisdek!" Jones exclaimed.

"Not Brouska. Damn. But a link?" Pulled his hair. Not the name he was looking for, but it was another link. He looked at the roof of the car again. He had a hunch. Tapped his cell.

"Max. When visitors come for lunch, do they have to show ID?"

"No. The resident signs them up and pays for the meal."

"What I would like to know is the name of the woman who comes to visit her. Dizzy? Grandniece? Any way you can find that out?"

"Give me five minutes and I'll call you back."

"Wait. Wait. No one can know. You can't say anything."

"Don't worry. Remember, IRS agent and Deputy Sheriff." She hung up laughing.

Damn. Double damn. She wouldn't do anything stupid would she? Should he call Stone? Five minutes, he'd give her five minutes. She couldn't get in too much trouble in five minutes, could she? He started the car but didn't shift into gear, counting off the minutes. He hadn't expected her to go DO something, just answer a question. It was taking too long.

His phone rang. Max, thank God.

"Got it," she said. "I'll text it. But first you have to tell me why."

Cav decided she'd be safer if she knew. "Mrs. Rydel went home this morning. Her house has been ransacked."

"Oh, that poor woman. Where is she? I'll go stay with her."

That would work, Cav thought with a smile. "Lori took her back to Forest. Go sit with both of them. And Max?"

"What?"

"The police are officially investigating this as an act of juvenile delinquency. We don't want anyone connecting it to other vandalized or destroyed homes."

"Got it. Mum's the word. I might need to tell Stone."

Well of course she would, he thought. Dancing? "Him only. No one else. Send me that name."

His cell dinged as soon as he disconnected, and he looked down. Saw part of an accounting page with Saturday, Lunch, and the date at the top. Under that a list of residents and guests for lunch.

Izzy Smith. Damn. "What kind of name is Smith?" he complained.

"Common American surname," Jones said.

"Common American alias," Cav corrected. "Run her."

"She doesn't exist," Jones said. "Not under Izzy Smith." He paused. "Wait. Let me check the arson report."

Maybe his intuition was growing up, Cav thought.

"Yes. Female acquaintance of owner. Izzy made the report. Izzy Burke, Burk with an e."

Was that closer to Brouska? Cav wondered. "Run that through our records." He saw Jones was on board now with the idea.

"Doing it."

They both watched the screen.

"Bingo. Name change. Three years ago. Was Brouskovetski. Changed her name to Burke."

"Yes. Knew there was a link. Knew it." Cav punched the air once.

"Let me check where Smith comes from."

Cav sat forward. "Let's go talk to Ida again. Um. No." He called Sally over to the squad car.

"Yes, Boss?"

"I want you to go to Forest. Talk to Ms. Rydel again." He turned to Jones. "Call your sister, tell her Sally wants to meet with them."

They waited.

"Lori will meet Sally at the door. But Boss, won't people know we're interested in Forest if we send a uniform?"

"We're sending a new hire. Inexperienced. Hesitant. Fumbling. Maybe useless. You handle that okay Sally?"

She hung her head. Her lips trembled. "Oh, Boss. I get to do real cop work? I'll try my best, Sir." She was laughing at him.

"We want to know how Ms. Rydel became sick three weeks ago. Who knew she was planning to go home? Whatever you can get us. Let her tell you. Lead the conversation into her expected visit. The rest of it? Sheriff's Office is not really interested. It's neighborhood kids trashing a house. We're just sending you so we can say we followed up. Got it?"

"Sure Boss. I'll try to be worthy of this honor."

Chavez had said Sally would be the next promotion and Cav thought he was right. She caught on quick.

"He burned down his own grandmother's house," Jones said disbelieving.

"Wouldn't put it past him. But we don't know she's his grandmother. Could be a great aunt, or just a friend of the family. A neighbor."

"And he found out she was in Forest and used her house. Knew she wasn't coming back. Sent Izzy – Niece? Grandniece? Sister? To watch her." Jones nodded and continued. "Then Izzy tells him the old lady is going home. He burns the place down because he can't clean it up."

"Yeah. Moves his operation into Ida's house. But this time he has a backup plan and he gets a warning she's going home. Coincidently, she gets sick, giving him time to hide his tracks. Can't have too many arsons. It would arouse suspicion."

He looked at Jones. "So where is Brouska now? Does this connection help us find him?" And how did Lucinda know Izzy had an unpronounceable name? Probably heard it during the argument the two women had over Grumpy going home. Did it matter?

Cav thought some more, gave up. Sally would get them something. Or Lori would.

*

Lori had kept up meaningless chatter on the way back to Forest while Ida wept continuously into her tissue. Lori helped her out of the car and held her arm as they walked to her apartment. Ida didn't want the nurse or sedatives, she just wanted to sit in her rocker. Lori sat quietly on the couch trying to think of some way to help.

Cav had been so gentle and patient with Ida. Holding her hand. Preparing her for disappointment while allowing her to hold out some hope her treasures could be salvaged. Lori couldn't believe anything would be recovered from the quick look she'd had into the entranceway and living room. The stink had been overpowering. The holes in the walls, the graffiti. Trash. She'd asked him before she left with Ida.

He'd shrugged, "Don't know. I wouldn't hold out much hope. Her pain will have eased in the two or three days it will take EDU to work through the evidence. We'll look," he promised.

EDU. Lori always thought of them as CSI no matter how many times Cav corrected her. CSI is what they were called on TV, and it made more sense than Evidence Detection Unit.

Max knocked and came in. "Cav asked me to stay with you both." She went over and sat by Ida, talking to her quietly. And the sobbing slowed down.

Lori's cell rang with Cav's tune. "Don't worry. I understand," she answered. "Don't mention drugs. Mob. Stick with neighborhood teenagers. Why would anyone do that?" She snorted and answered her own question. "Because they're slime. Dirtbags. Destroy an old lady's cherished possessions. Memories. It's so sad."

"We'll get them honey. We'll get them because you came to me with your suspicions. Because of that, we know this isn't simple teenage vandalism. We have a lead. Jones and I are following up."

"Thanks for sending Max. She's a wonder. She has calming techniques I've never even heard of. Ida didn't want a sedative. Doesn't want to lie down. Max had a solution. Shot of bourbon in the coffee." Lori laughed. "For all of us. Thanks."

"Don't get her snockered. I sent Sally to interview her. Find out who knew she was going home a month ago. And how she got sick."

"You don't think someone harmed her on purpose?" Lori asked shocked. Then when he was silent. "You do." She exhaled. "Of course, someone did. Don't worry. Between the three of us, we'll get you names. I want you to hang whoever did that to her house."

Cav wanted to also.

\*

He was smiling when he hung up. Lori was angry now. Both at the manufactured illness and at the destruction of Ida's home.

He loved her. Wondered what it was that flipped him out of like and lust into love. Well maybe not out of lust. Or like. He still lusted and liked.

So what moved him up into love. He was a detective, wasn't he? What was it about her that made him fall in love? She was beautiful. But it wasn't just looks. He'd liked her the minute he met her. And then was impressed by the way she'd faced Becca down. Took a brave person to tell Becca what to do. But Lori told Becca what to do and then made her do it. Of course, Becca was recuperating from the shooting and relearning how to walk, and she wanted to get well so it wasn't a real battle, just circling for who would be boss. Lori won every time. He liked that. Respected that. And Lori and Becca had become fast friends.

Is that what he loved? Her ability to turn a cranky client into a healthy client and a best friend? No. It was her inner need to turn an injured victim into a healthy happy person.

He shook his head. Business Cav, he told himself. He sat for another minute.

"Let's walk through the house again." He led the way, waited at the door until Bruce saw them and hurried over.

"Might have something for you." He held out a plastic bag. With a receipt.

Cav held it up to the flashlight. Turned it both ways. Looked at Bruce with an eyebrow raised. "Can't read it."

"Receipt."

"Yeah."

"Dated four weeks ago. Before the drug dealers abandoned the place."

"So, not the kids."

"Pretty sure."

"Get anything off it besides the date?"

"Working on that. Have some new apps on my tablet, that's how I got the date. These apps are powerful. Testing them out, actually. Can do a lot of it right here, don't even have to go to the lab. Will do a better job there of course and document everything. Hold on. Let's take this outside." One of his men held the receipt and Bruce fiddled with buttons and sliding screens talking to himself. If Bruce could get them the name of the store and the time, Cav might be able to find out who. It would be worth the wait.

He started to walk away but Bruce stopped him. "Hold on. I can get you some more." He fiddled with the tablet buttons again. Cav wasn't sure what he was after. How many sandwiches? What kind? Neither would have much importance. Might tell them how many people were at the house. He waited. Not patiently. Looked around for anything salvageable. Noticed a glass paperweight. Tapped Bruce on the elbow. "Is that broken?"

Bruce looked up, distracted. "What?" He looked where Cav was pointing. "No. You can pick it up. All this trash is mapped, photographed, and dusted. Found some pretty good prints on the paperweight. Wife has something like that. Cost a fortune. Part of a pair." Again he looked around absently. "Didn't find the mate."

"Let me have it, to return to the owner. It will give her hope."

"What? Oh, sure, sure. Betty? Do what the Sheriff wants." He went back to pushing buttons and sliding screens.

After ten minutes, Bruce said, "Ah ha. Here it is. Knew I could do it." With pride he held the image up. "Date, Time, store name." He paused. "Can't get if it's cash or credit, sorry. Maybe in the lab. More Eats is the name of the place."

He looked up at Cav. "Lousy food there."

"Yeah. I know the place. Think they serve leftover prison food. Didn't they go out of business?"

"Hm. No. Changed hands is all."

Cav clapped him on the back. "Great. Yes sir. You send me

whatever you get as soon as you get it. Come on Jones. Let's go get an early lunch."

Jones was only a half-step behind. Ten-thirty, but Cav could eat anytime, anything. And he knew where he would be getting his next meal.

They drove four blocks down the street until Jones spotted the shop. "New name, On-Line Café. Fresh paint, sparkling windows. Banner advertising new owner, Joe Johnson, new manager. Not going to find anything here," he complained.

"Might's well go in and check out the food."

The place was clean with a lunch counter and four high-tops. Two men eating at the counter, two high-tops occupied. The rest of the space devoted to computer stations. Most occupied.

Jones looked surprised when the new owner turned out to also be their server. And he was talkative. So they learned a lot. "Serve lunch from ten-thirty to three-thirty. After that snacks and cold sandwiches are available for my web surfers, until six when we close. Unlike a coffee shop, the customers are required to purchase both food and time on-line." He handed them menus and set down water. "Let me recommend the Reubens. My specialty. Backups are grilled cheese with tomato or roasted eggplant and tomato."

Cav cringed when he heard eggplant and ordered the Reuben. Jones found a chickpea and chicken salad on the menu. Cav cringed again, although, you know, that didn't sound too bad. Had chicken in it. And probably mayonnaise.

"Nice place you got here, Joe," Cav said when the man brought their sandwiches and sides.

"Yeah. I got the best of both worlds. The internet café is for the bank. That pays the bills. Lunch is for me. I love making lunch. Making sandwiches for hungry internet customers. Then I clean up and go to my second job, on-line podcasting. Never leave the building."

"How do you keep the keyboards clean?" Cav asked. His were

crumb holders, while they survived. Spilt coffee had already killed one this year. He tried not to eat or drink when he was using his tablet, but...

"Plastic covers. Go Look."

Cav did and decided he needed one. "Notice you have cameras." He pointed to one mounted in the corner.

"Yeah, I added them three months ago when I took over. Top of the line. Have enough cloud storage for forty-five days." He looked around the room. "Everything is updated or new. Only thing I kept from the old store was the bookkeeping system, since I designed it. If it ain't broke, don't fix it."

Cav's cell beeped right as he was getting ready to order dessert. He checked. "Ryan has information. Wants a meet at the gatehouse in an hour with DEA." He took the last bite of his sandwich and asked the owner, "Can we get—" he did a quick calculation in his head, "—a dozen of those premade sandwiches to go? Add an assortment of sides." He looked longingly at the cakes and pies. "And desserts, a dozen. We got drinks." And if he knew this crew, the drinks would be coffee. Except Gibbs who would drink tea.

Jones asked on the way out. "We're not asking about the sales slip?"

"Not yet. We check with the DEA team leader first, before we step in it. If it's our perps, we don't want anyone to know we're looking. This guy, Joe, comes across honest. But run him. Let's go talk to the Feds."

Becca, Kevin, and Ryan were waiting along with DEA Agent Dawson and his coordinator. Each grabbed a sandwich. Cav got another for himself, hesitated when he noticed the grilled cheese had tomato slices, but how bad could it be?

Dawson started the meeting with the obvious. "We cut your people loose from the farmhouse. Kept your surveillance rig. We appreciate the help. Although, Kevin here—" he shook his head, "—a piece of work. Guy's trying to sell me a house, for God's sake, in the middle of this. Although, we are pregnant, and the wife is dropping hints about a bigger place. One with a yard. Perspective is different with a kid on the way."

"Congratulations," Cav said.

A wide grin divided Dawson's face. "Yeah. I do good work. We're planning one of each. Big house, two kids, and a dog."

Cav had a vision of Lori pregnant, a little girl holding her hand, both watching a golden lab romp in the yard. He shook his head. Tonight. Tonight. He'd ask her tonight. She had to say yes. She had to. And then Kevin could find them a house.

Abashed at the image, Cav said, "We found a connection between Forest and the drugs and Brouska."

"If you did, you're the only one. We can't, and we've tried."

"There's an old lady at Forest. Russian. Has lived at Forest eight months. One day her nurse said she was well enough to go home. Big loud fight with her grandniece, or granddaughter, or maybe the woman is a caregiver. Anyhow, old Russian lady remains adamant and grandniece leaves angry. Old lady's house burns down that night. The fire, arson, is our only verified fact. The rest is gossip, and our single unidentified source to the argument is not totally reliable." He paused, thinking that was a benign description of Lucinda.

"I do not have that arson on my spreadsheet," Gibbs said.

"I know. It was before Max got there and while Stone was in the hospital. And the residents don't like the Russian. Call her Grumpy. I'm thinking she doesn't speak much English, but I haven't talked to her yet. Her house could be the first drug house."

He continued. "The grandniece is Izzy Burke, with an 'e'. Or Izzy Smith. Before a legal name change, she was Izolda, spelling last name, B-r-o-u-s-k-o-v-e-t-s-k-i."

Gibbs's feet hit the floor. He'd been sitting with them on his desk. Cav smiled at Jones who grinned back.

"There is no such thing as coincidence," Gibbs said.

"Agreed. But we couldn't find anything else in our records under Izolda Burke. No address or phone either. We did find her as Izzy Burke in the arson report. I have my people researching the arson investigation. Burke has two assaults, no charges."

Gibbs was typing. "We don't show Izolda." And Dawson nodded to his man, James Marshall, to check their files.

Dawson said, "Hmmm. So you think, what? The old lady fell or got beat up and sent to rehab. Her kid? Grandniece, whatever, is related to Brouska, and he uses her vacant place to sell his drugs. When it looks like the old gal will be sent home, he burns the place down? Burns down this woman's house?"

"Maybe, something like that. Don't really like that scenario, but it makes sense. Now, the old lady is at Forest and the 'niece' notices how some folks own homes and those homes are empty for long periods of time. Izzy passes that information on to her Uncle Brouska. We're following up on that."

"I'll have our people pursue the familial connection," Gibbs said.

"We couldn't find anything to tie her to Brouska except the name."

"I'll talk to ICE and Immigration. They entered the country sometime under visas."

"Okay, FBI will follow up on Brouska," Dawson said. "Meanwhile, the reason I called this meeting is that the DEA will be hitting the sale houses tomorrow at three."

Kevin asked, "Why?"

"Best time. We discussed hitting the pill factory at dawn, before anyone is up and around, but decided against it because it leaves too much time for the bust to leak. The dealers are really busy at three in the afternoon and we want as many buyers and sellers as we can get. We don't want to have to go back again next week."

Cav said, "Seems like you'll be up against more felons with guns, though."

Dawson shrugged. "We have overwhelming manpower between the Feds, staties, and the locals, your guys included. Show of force should be enough to disillusion even the craziest crook. They'll be outmanned and outgunned."

"Got her," Becca said into the silence.

"Who?" Dawson asked.

"Izolda Brouskovetski, Smith, Burke with an 'e'. Izolda was married to one, John Smith, for four months. Smith was found full of bullet holes in an alley. Believed to be drug related. Case is still open. Mrs. Smith took a new name, Burke." Becca held up her finger. "And, she owns a house on Warren Ave."

"Huh. We need a team out there now," Cav said. He turned to Dawson. "You got all my SWAT teams and equipment, Dawson. Can I get some back?"

Dawson shook his head. "All tied up in the interagency action tomorrow. Everyone has an assigned task. If you want to go in that house, you have to do it with the people you have. And you have to do it at three. Any sooner and something might leak. And after our guys bust the sale houses, it will be too late for you. Even if nothing leaks, the media will show up as soon as they get word of the busts. You have probable cause; I'll get warrants to enter and search. You already have warrants for Eggert and Brouska."

"I got equipment," Kevin said. "Enough to outfit six men with cameras, audio, and video. You can run surveillance form RV 2. She's a smaller version of RV SPY. A baby rig. But you'll need me to operate the equipment," he added gleefully. "John and I have been working on infrared. Got FLIR thermal imaging cameras loaded on a couple of drones we can fly."

"Does it work?"

"Oh, yeah."

"How do you know?" Dawson asked.

"Tested it."

"How? Where?"

"We didn't do anything illegal. Tested it on my house, here, Jake's office and garage. Jake's married to my sister. Runs a security business. FLIR works great. We can tell you how many people are in the house."

Cav pulled his hair, looked at Kevin a moment, considered, then smiled. It could work. Cav raised an eyebrow at Gibbs who snorted. Feigning disgust, he stood up.

"Stand up," he told Kevin who looked concerned but rose bravely to his feet.

"Raise your right hand."

A grin replaced the worried look when Ryan swore him in. "You are a sworn agent of the FBI for this operation only. No badge. Don't even ask. No weapon. Understand?"

"Yes, Sir," Kevin snapped with a salute and then danced around the room.

"Already regretting this," Gibbs grumbled.

"We need him," Cav said, "and his equipment. He'll settle down."

Cav counted men in his head. He could get eight, including himself. Not all would need to be wired. Cav's men had body cams. Maybe Kevin had more equipment hidden away.

"I'm in," Becca said. "Maybe Joey, if you need." Their other brother.

Gibbs laughed. "And I have compatible equipment for us."

Dawson stood. "We'll get you a warrant so there'll be no problem at trial. Tomorrow, 3 pm," he said as he went out the door.

Cav frowned. "Okay folks, we got work to do. The girl will be with the old lady at Forest. Shouldn't be anyone in the house." He paused. "But I'm betting there will be two men. It's a perfect place for them to hide out. Kevin, I need that van now. Just get in place and as soon as the warrant comes in set up cameras. Sound too, if you can manage. And the infrared. Drones. The works."

Kevin rubbed his chin. "Depends on how far away we set up and how close I can get a mic for sound. Infrared too." He motioned to the monitor on the wall. He'd brought up the house on his real estate site. It was a two-story red brick with many gables. Cav didn't understand this trend for so many points. They made him irritated and uneasy and edgy. His sister lived in a house with ten gables, though, and she didn't seem to have any problem. The two simple well-placed gables on his blue house might be old fashioned but he found them comforting. He snorted. 'His house?' Fat chance.

Dizzy's mansion was described as eight bedroom, seven and a half bath, with media room and game room. He doubted he'd ever need a game room. Shoot pool at home? Pool was for a bar and friends. The house also had an infinity pool, jacuzzi, and tennis court.

There was a floor plan and pictures of each room. And video. Cav snorted. His office had tried to convince realtors not to share so much information on social media, but apparently, buyers wanted floor plans and photos. But today the advertising worked in their favor. The house had sold furnished six months ago and it was very possible it still looked the same inside.

Kevin said, "Brick will interfere with sound." He held up a hand. "I'll do what I can. Overhead drones."

"Okay. When you have your end ready to go, call me. Gibbs and I will be at my office working on a plan for personnel and equipment."

Back at the office, Chavez had spoken with DEA. "Dawson has a good guy in charge of logistics, coordinating all the localities, supplies, entities. He's got everyone working together. Makes it look easy." He sipped his coffee.

"I've talked with a couple of the local cops I know, Green in New Jersey and Hardy Warrington in D.C.; they're good men. Already been contacted and attached to DEA. They sent in extra men to help keep the scumbags under 24-hour surveillance, recording everything. Gibbs sent FBI teams out to each location for backup. Enough manpower to follow the buyers. We'll know where the perps are when we're ready. There is a printout on your desk of each county."

"Good. Good." Cav tugged his hair.

Chavez continued with some gossip. "You'll be happy to know Dawson sent what looks like a whole squad as back-up to the farm. The Specialists. They're working directly with Jones."

"The BOLOs we issued as 'do not approach or apprehend' paid off. We've located all but one vehicle, and DEA has those under surveillance."

"Which one are we missing? Eggert?"

Chavez nodded. "Yeah. Still looking. He's got to be near here." He put up a map, showing locations and agents on each drug vehicle.

"I think we got him. And Brouska." Cav told him what they discovered and the plan, bringing a wide smile to his face.

And the planning kept them busy through the afternoon and evening when they ordered-in dinner. They had to cover every contingency, including, hopefully, the presence of both Brouska and Eggert. Something always went wrong; didn't matter how well you planned. Cav just hoped they had those screwups covered. They picked men available from his office and the FBI and notified them to be ready for a special op. Equipment was collected and laid out on the long conference table in his office.

Cav touched base with his counterparts in the adjacent states and dealt with schedule changes necessitated by the op.

Kevin called in. Infra-red had located five warm bodies in the house. Four men, one woman. So they went back over their plans and then, finally, went home.

Lori was at the kitchen counter when he let himself in. She looked at him with a start, stiffened, and quickly gathered the papers she'd been working on and shoved them under a pile. Again. But upside down.

He kept his face carefully blank. Didn't let the slap show.

"You're home earlier than I expected," she said, uneasily.

He checked his watch. Twenty minutes earlier than he'd estimated when he called and told her to go ahead and eat. They'd worked on plans for another two hours.

"Burned out."

He walked toward her, and she pulled her calendar over the papers. That stopped him in his tracks.

"What's going on Lori?"

"Nothing. Nothing. Just like you, working on schedules. For tomorrow."

A lie. He was an investigator; he knew a lie when he heard it. She wasn't hiding schedules. He could have looked through her things anytime, but you don't spy on the woman you love. You wait. Wait for her to talk to you. Lie to you?

She stood and walked to a cupboard. Took down a glass which she filled with water. Looked at the sink with great interest.

"Lori, talk to me." He strode over, touched her shoulder, and she spun around almost spilling the water.

"What's wrong honey?"

"I don't know what you mean. Just edgy I guess." She held the glass with both hands. Walked around him and sat back down.

"Maybe if you tell me what the problem is, I can help."

"You can't help," she said.

"Okay." What did he say now? Christ, he spent his whole career interrogating people. He should be able to ask simple questions. But he was afraid he'd ask the wrong question. Get the wrong answer. The one he dreaded.

She straightened the edges of the sheets. Wouldn't look at him. This was the woman he loved, and she wouldn't look at him.

"Well," he said, not sure what he was going to say. Not really wanting to say anything. Just wanting things back the way they were.

She jumped up, almost knocking the chair over. "You can't help. You're the problem," she blurted.

There it was. Out in the open. The look on her face hit him in the gut. The tears in her eyes hit him in the heart.

"I'm the problem," he repeated softly.

She nodded.

"I thought you loved me. What happened?"

Her mouth worked. Nothing came out.

He waited. But all she did was shake her head back and forth.

He sighed. "If you don't want me here, I'll pack my stuff and be gone." He hadn't intended to say that.

She stared at him with her mouth open now. Still no words came out.

He headed for the bedroom, but she pushed in front of him. Blocked him. He waited.

"No," she said fiercely. "No." Shook her head. Waved her hand. "No."

"You don't trust me even to get my stuff?" he asked shocked.

"No. Yes. Stop. Dammit you're confusing me," she stammered, wiping the tears.

"Well then, that makes two of us."

He waited. A long minute which felt like an hour. He was breathing through his nose. Eyeing her. Waiting.

She shook her head. Just once. Looked down at her hands. Turned away.

"Talk to me, Lori. How am I the problem?"

She stiffened her back, turned around to face him, raised her head. Opened her mouth to speak. Nothing came out. She tried again. Stared at him. Shook her head and turned away.

"Is there another man?"

She spun back. "Don't be silly. Of course not."

That was good. And she'd found her voice. He waited.

"Oh, I am so messed up," she uttered in despair and then said those dreaded words which always preceded a breakup.

"It's not you," she said and paused. Finished the phrase. "It's me."

His stomach tightened like he'd been sucker punched. That's what they said when they broke up with you.

"Okay then." He felt his shoulders sag. Closed his eyes. "You want me to send for my stuff?"

"No. Stop!" she yelled. "Just be quiet. Wait. Just wait. Give me a few minutes."

Reprieve? He could wait. Silently. Three minutes.

"Let me help. Tell me what I can do to make it right."

She nodded once sharply, pulled out the papers and threw them at his chest. "Look at these."

"You sure?" he asked catching them.

"Yes. Look. Read."

He read the first page; didn't understand. Looked at her to make sure she wanted him to go on and she motioned with her hand he should continue. He did, skimming the rest of the pages. Didn't understand. They had nothing to do with him. Pulled his hair.

"I don't understand. Why did you hide them? Why couldn't you show me?"

"Because it means a new path. One different from what I had planned."

"So? Forest has offered you a sub-contract position. What's the problem? Looks fairly straight forward. Did you talk to an attorney?"

"That's why I didn't show you."

"The attorney told you not to show me?"

"No."

"What did he say?"

"I haven't talked to an attorney."

Oh.

"Are you considering the offer? It sounds pretty good. Your own physical therapy division at Forest. They supply all the equipment, a secretary to schedule appointments and track income and expenses and do the tax work. You hate doing that. You take care of physical therapy for their residents while keeping your own clients. Sounds good."

"See. There. See," she complained. "That there, right there, is why I didn't show you."

"What?" he asked completely confused now.

"You have opinions."

He tugged his hair.

She said, "I wanted to ask you."

He waited. Then asked, "Ask me what?"

"What I should do."

"Why didn't you?"

"Because I wanted your opinion."

He tugged his hair so hard; he pulled some out. Ouch.

"You're not making any sense, Lori."

"Of course, I'm not making any sense. Don't you think I know that? That's what you do to me." She stomped around the kitchen.

It was his turn to stand with his mouth open. The words didn't make any sense. He raised both hands getting ready to say something, but she beat him to it.

"I suddenly realized that your opinion was important. That I wanted to talk it over with you. That scared me. I've always made

my own decisions. Never needed anyone else's opinion. 'Til you."
She looked him in the eye. "'Til you," she whispered.

And suddenly it clicked. Relief filled his heart. He laughed.
"You love me."

She burst into tears. He stepped to her and gathered her into his
arms, rubbing her back. "Shush. Shush," he murmured gently. "It's
okay. It's okay. I love you too."

He lifted her chin, Pushed her hair away from her face. Holding
her eyes with his he repeated, "I love you, too." He wiped the tears
with his thumb. Licked his thumb, tasted the tears. They both
stilled. He leaned down and kissed her, elated when she kissed him
back. He picked her up and carried her to the bedroom.

The words simply slipped out while they made slow sweet love.
"Marry me," he said.

Her eyes popped open. The dreamy look on her face vanished,
replaced with shock.

Uh, oh.

"Marry me?" he asked.

"Of course," she said and pulled him in tighter, laughed. "You'll
propose to me again in the morning."

Looked at her. "What? Why? You accepted," he said with a satisfied smirk.

"Because we can't tell our kids the X-rated version when they
ask, how did Daddy propose?"

He had a quick image of that little curly headed girl again, the
one who looked like Lori and laughed with her.

# SATURDAY

And he did propose, over morning coffee. He made it. He got down on his knee with the ring. Traditional. He had a moment of worry she wouldn't like the ring. "My grandmother's." Then he started to say they could pick a ring out together, but she grabbed it from him and held it to her chest, tears in her eyes, and made him slip it on her finger. A perfect fit.

Before he left, he warned her they were looking at Izzy, and she should keep her distance. Kissed her, stroked her finger with the ring.

He went directly to Kevin's RV Baby where he and Ryan watched several monitors. RV Baby wasn't anything like RV SPY. A Thor motor coach which looked like a delivery van. Smaller, with a skinny central aisle and every square inch of space packed with equipment. Its only concession to surveilling humans was a tiny bathroom in a corner. Electronics were even attached to the outer door. The skylight in the roof was the only other area not covered with electronics. It was a tight fit for the five people now inside.

One monitor picked up the DEA transmission from the Estates house, another from the farmhouse. The remaining monitors showed different views of Izzy's house. Chavez said, "Interesting people going in and out of Izzy's overnight." He put pictures up on another monitor. Named the faces. "All known dealers. They're meeting with someone inside the house, but we haven't had any visuals of that person."

"You think it's Brouska? Or Eggert?"

Chavez tilted his head and frowned. "Really no way to tell. Someone important. The woman lives there; we've seen her a couple of times. She's been in and out. Not there now, so these men are not meeting her. Someone else in the house."

"This guy—" Chavez put up another photo, "—is answering the door. Has both federal and state warrants out on him."

"Anyone else in the house that we know of?"

"Maid and housekeeper came in this morning and left at one. We have identified two bodyguards." He put their pictures alongside the doorman. "Both wanted. Armed. Guarding someone."

"Four then. We're taking them down. Izzy won't be there; we can always get her later."

"I want Eggert," Ryan said.

"Curtains drawn on all the windows," Kevin announced, though Cav could see that for himself. "No cameras out front by the door. That's really weird."

"No. In a way it makes sense. If you have an assortment of crooks and mob bosses coming to visit, they probably wouldn't want to be photographed."

"Hadn't thought of that. And no one is going to rob Brouska."

They fine-tuned the plan. All knew their parts. Kevin would stay with RV Baby and keep everyone appraised of status.

A 'GOPARTY' truck pulled up to the sidewalk in front of the house and parked. The driver hopped out, walked around to the back of the truck and raised the back doors. He climbed in and a minute later dropped a wheeled dolly out the door.

The op had begun. Cav gave one last quick glance to the monitor of Stone's farm where a SWAT truck had just pulled up at the front door, a second truck was at the back door, and two more bookended the barn. SWAT, DEA, and FBI were piling out of the vehicles.

Hazardous Materials Response Unit was standing by at the barn. He could just identify Jones with the HAZMAT Unit.

He'd catch the video later. Now he turned his attention to the brick house as the GO PARTY guy dropped down beside his dolly, pulled two boxes from the bed of the truck, and slid them on the hand truck. He dragged the dolly the four feet up the front walkway and then up three steps to the front door and checked his clipboard against the house number. The delivery person, a woman it was obvious now since he could see Sally's long blond hair. She gave them a wide smile as she looked back at the street, sending them her view in both directions. For a brief instant the nose of RV Baby appeared on the monitor. She took a breath and rang the doorbell. Waited and rang again.

Looked all around. Yelled, "Delivery!" Peeked at the front windows, heavily covered with curtains on this sunny day. She leaned to the left and then the right toward both sides of the building. She rang again.

A muffled curse answered from inside and the cover of the peephole in the center of the door slid open.

"What?" a scratchy male voice asked from inside.

"Delivery."

"Leave it there."

"Can't. You have to sign."

"Take it back."

"Can't, perishable."

"Your problem."

"Look, mister. You contracted for this delivery. Paid upfront. Now I can leave these boxes on your stoop here or take them back to the warehouse along with the ones still on my truck where they will be disposed of. Up to you."

She looked at her clipboard. "Um, I got Maine lobster, Florida stone crabs, caviar. Ooh a whole case of 30-year-old Laphroaig. You know what, mister? I think you're right. I'll just take this all back. Employees get to share refused deliveries." She made to turn around.

"Hey. Leave that stuff."

"Can't. I told you. I need a signature." She started down a step.

"I'll say you didn't come."

She laughed. "Got that covered, mister." She pointed to her shirt pocket. "Body cam. Recorded everything. You want this stuff or not?"

They heard the door locks click. Three of them. And the door swung open revealing an ugly thickset man with greasy hair.

"That's Bruno, Brouska's right hand man," Ryan breathed.

The hulk reached to grab her handheld tablet. "Let me sign."

She pulled it out of his reach. "After everything is in the house. I can roll them back to the kitchen near your refrigerator. Part of the service. But, just for you, I can leave them here on the stoop, and you can take them back after I leave. They're pretty heavy."

He looked at the large boxes, struggled to lift the top one, but they'd packed it with ice over bricks. He gave up and waved her in, looked up the street before following her and closing the door.

"Nice entryway," she said making sure the body cam caught the eight-foot square entranceway with inner glass doors which was the same as the floor plan online.

"Straight back."

"Got it." She started down the hall, keeping her head tilted down, while looking all around sending images to the monitors in the truck. The camera was in her cap, not her pocket. She sidetracked to the left through a wide archway and started down the corridor where Kevin's spanking new infrared gizmo showed warm bodies.

"Stop," the hood yelled, and she took another two steps forward before she turned her head slowly to look at him, puzzled.

"That's the wrong way," he said.

She looked all around slowly, dully. "Oh. Which door?"

"Back this way." He motioned her back the way she had come

as another man stepped through an open door to her left. "What's going on, Bruno?"

"Delivery. Lady made a wrong turn heading for the kitchen, Alex."

"Sorry." Sally said giving him a wide smile. "What? Back this way?" she asked Bruno.

"Yeah, lady."

The man in the doorway, frowned, looked Sally up and down, dismissed her as not a problem. "Get it done. Get her out of here." He turned back into the room.

She watched him stalk away. "Not very friendly. Grouch," she said just loud enough for Bruno to hear and headed for the kitchen. Did a slow survey of the room. Two windows, door to garage, back door—French doors with a simple bolt. She walked to the refrigerator and started to pull her dolly out from under the boxes. The top box slipped and began to fall. They both reached for it, but Bruno was successful. He stopped it and shoved it back up.

While his back was turned, Sally unbolted the door.

"Oh, thank goodness. That one is breakable." She moved the dolly to slide the box onto the counter then unloaded the bottom package and headed back for the front door. He hurried after her. "Hey, I sign now," he demanded.

"Got more boxes to bring in, then you can sign," she said and stopped at the door. "If you're in such a hurry you could help, it will go quicker."

"Your job," he said with a snarl and stood on the stoop watching as she struggled two heavy boxes onto her hand truck, balancing two smaller ones precariously on top. Back at the entrance she dragged the hand truck past him and pushed the door fully open but still got her dolly stuck in the doorway. It tipped, sending boxes flying.

The goon jumped out of the way. "What the hell? Clumsy bitch."

Sally struggled to keep the dolly upright. "Can you get those for me? she asked motioning to the ones just outside as she fought with the dolly.

He backed further onto the stoop. "Get them yourself, bitch."

She spun, grabbed his arm and pulled it toward her, and using her momentum, she pushed him face first into the wall, holding him there with her hand braced on his back between his shoulders.

"Police. You're under arrest," she said into this ear.

"What? You can't do that. Come busting in here. You got no cause."

"Outstanding arrest warrant," she said and, twisting his arm up and back, she forced him down on the ground.

Cav, Ryan, Becca, and four cops rushed from the vehicles parked around the corner. Cav said to Mike, "Search him, cuff him, stuff him in the van. Cuff him to the bar." Cav couldn't believe Kevin had added a secure bar in RV Baby. Sally pulled off her delivery shirt revealing her deputy uniform.

Two cops went around back and, as soon as Mike returned, they went in, weapons drawn. Each person had an assigned hall and rooms to clear. They had gone over the plan a dozen times. Becca headed to the east wing. Chavez headed upstairs with three men. Infrared showed those rooms empty, but they had to clear them. Cav, Ryan, and Sally edged through the archway toward the infrared images. Cleared each room as they passed and braced the doorway to the billiards room.

Cav peeked in. Saw Brouska and Eggert shooting pool. Alex was at the bar watching three basketball games on the large screen.

Eggert was ragging on Brouska. "When you miss that shot, the game is mine. You might as well pay up. That's the third game today. Maybe you should take up Hearts or Go Fish."

"I ain't made the shot yet," Brouska replied.

Both men were standing on the near side of the pool table their backs to the door holding their cue sticks.

Gibbs and Cav stepped in, splitting up. Ryan took two steps to Alex and said, "Don't move, Alex."

Cav and Sally mirrored the act with Brouska and Eggert. "You heard him. Police. You are all under arrest."

Both men spun around.

"I said," Cav repeated. "Drop the cue sticks."

Eggert gripped his tightly, anger mottling his face.

"Bullet's faster than a cue stick," Cav said quietly. "You don't want to be shot resisting arrest. Drop the cue sticks."

"Okay, dropping the cue stick," Eggert said, letting it fall to the floor.

Brouska set his stick on the pool table. "What are you doing in here? You can't come into my house without a warrant."

"Have a warrant." Cav nodded to Sally who held up a group of documents. "Your house?" Cav said. "Funny, I thought the house was in Izzy's name."

"Izzy don't own anything." He sneered.

"You sure?" Cav asked and took the warrant from Sally. Turned to the back page. Nodded. "Um, owner, one Izzy Smith. Who is she?" He shook his head. "Doesn't matter."

"If you have her name on the warrant, you're all messed up. My lawyers will tear you to shreds. You can't come busting into my home."

Cav continued as if he hadn't heard him. "And the search warrant is for the residence at this address. Doesn't mention owner. And, more important, we have arrest warrants for both of you."

Eggert snickered smugly. "You don't know nothing. I'll be out in a hour. You're just a stupid copper if you think Izzy owns this place."

Copper? Who used that term anymore? Cav wondered. "We don't really need to know if she does, since this address is on the warrant. Just the address. All nicely filled out and signed."

"Fool." Eggert sniggered at the same time Brouska bellowed, "Shut up, Eggert."

Eggert stared at him in shock.

"I want a lawyer. Now. We don't say nothin' without a lawyer," Brouska stated with another warning look at Eggert.

"You can call a lawyer as soon as you get downtown. Hands on top of your heads." Cav waited for them to comply. "Now turn around slowly and face the table. My deputy is going to handcuff you and frisk you."

Chavez came in with three deputies.

"Yeah, yeah. You won't get away with this. I'll have your jobs."

"Yeah, Yeah," Cav agreed. The deputies collected weapons (two guns from each of the three men). Wallets and cell phones were placed on the pool table. "Take them downtown. Process them. Put them in a holding cell." He looked at his watch. They were right on time. DEA should have finished with their raids. "Let them call their attorney."

Cav watched them leave, both complaining loudly.

"Okay. We search. Drugs, cash, books." Even crooks had to keep account books. "Sally, get the cell phones to the lab, I want to know who they've been talking to." He especially hoped for links to the farmhouse and stash house. "I want to know who this house belongs to. We're missing something. Eggert was pretty sure of himself on the ownership issue. Gibbs and I will start here. The rest of you know your assignments. Glove up. Get to it."

They didn't find any paperwork in the game room.

Disgusted, Cav walked over to the rack holding the pool cues. "Nice setup." He touched the rack. "Extra heavy duty," he mumbled to himself and tugged on it. Felt around the edges. Something clicked and the whole wall rack slid to the side revealing a hidden door. He opened it and stared openmouthed at the twelve- by twenty-foot room, the walls covered with rifles and handguns.

"Wow."

"What?" Gibbs asked, turning from the cabinets under the bar. "Oh, that is quite an armory. Looks like they are planning for a war. Is that a bazooka? I'll call for Special Weapons to help." Gibbs pulled out his phone and arranged more men while Cav walked slowly around the room. "Must be a couple hundred weapons here. Handguns, rifles, ammo."

Becca hollered from upstairs, "You guys are gonna want to see this."

"Think she can match this armory?" Cav asked as they headed up.

"Yeah," Ryan said as they both looked in the door.

"Huh," Cav said. Ryan was right.

They were looking at an office. A stylish, feminine office. Dainty rosewood desk in the center of the room. A two-drawer file cabinet beside it, also rosewood. A small, floral camelback sofa with a dozen pillows. Matching desk chair. Cav had never seen a floral desk chair before. He touched it, leather. It rocked. The surface of the desk was clear of papers with only a Tiffany lamp (real?), a fancy pen holder, and a photograph of Izzy and an unknown male. A life-sized portrait of Izzy hung on the wall. Painted. Four by six, Cav guessed. Looked better than her mug shot.

He turned his attention to the desk, pulled a drawer handle. Locked. He tried all the drawers. Be stupid not to try them all only to find one unlocked tomorrow. He bumped into Becca when he straightened from the bottom drawers. "All locked."

"I can open 'em," Becca offered.

He thought about it for all of two seconds. The drawers were locked. He had a signed search warrant. Becca worked for the FBI. And Becca had good hands. He'd seen her open locks before.

"Okay. Get it printed first."

Her face lit up and she pulled tools out of her pocket. "Won't touch anything."

"You carry those around with you?" he asked surprised. They were kind of illegal.

"Yeah." She snorted. "How did you think I was going to open the locks?"

Gibbs ignored them and walked across the room to stand in front of the portrait of Izzy. "Who would have thought she could clean up like this. She looked really bad in her mug shots. This is almost regal."

Cav came over and stood behind him. Becca wouldn't open the drawers any faster with him watching.

"Eyes. Man. Look at her eyes. Mean. Angry. Artist couldn't do anything with them." Gibbs studied the painting. He leaned closer.

"Eggert was right. We are stupid coppers. Look at the date." He tapped the picture. "This was painted thirty years ago. It's the old lady. Grumpy."

"We should have guessed. We knew this operation was too slick for it to be Eggert. He's muscle. Brouska is an empty-headed bully. And Izzy never fit, not enough history. The old lady is the brains. And the old lady's right where she needs to be to know about abandoned properties. All she has to do is stand around and listen." He'd thought the old lady's anger was simply from being abandoned in a nursing home, but maybe it had been directed at Jones. Everyone knew he was a cop. Did Grumpy know Cav and Gibbs were also cops? Cav had a bad feeling in his gut, pulled his hair. "Shit. Lori." He pulled out his cell. Hit a button, held it nervously to his ear.

Jorge came in, the first of Cav's EDU team to arrive, and started to dust everything for fingerprints.

"Damn. Voicemail." Cav glared at his cell. Lori sometimes did turn her phone off when she was working with a patient. But why did that have to be right now. He couldn't remember her schedule. Hadn't really looked at it. Shit. Left a terse voicemail message. "Call me. Emergency."

Gibbs tapped the picture with a knuckle. It moved.

Cav's eyes widened as Gibbs slid the frame to the right, on

tracks like the cue stick rack, revealing a safe with a digital electronic keypad.

He whistled then turned to look at the guy fingerprinting the desk. "Jorge, you need to dust this panel when you finish with the desk."

"Almost done. Only one set of prints here. All too small to be a man."

Cav tugged his hair, tried Lori again. Left a text, same message. Maybe she would get that. He didn't like the idea of her being in the same building with that woman. If the guy who had painted this portrait had caught the correct emotion in the eyes, Lori could be in danger. And Cav thought the artist had. The woman was a mob boss. She ran a five-state drug-running operation. Probably more than drugs. She wasn't a lightweight.

"Call Max," Gibbs suggested.

He pulled up Max's number. Voicemail again. Left the same message. He didn't like it.

"Damn. Both went to voicemail."

Jorge came over to stare at the painting with them. Moved to the safe. "Desk is dusted. And I dusted the chair and under the desk." Then he added with a grin, "The pretty lady picked the lock."

They hurried over. Becca was already opening the center drawer with gloved hands. "Laptop in here," she said not touching it.

Jorge came over and dusted the laptop. Opened it and dusted the interior too while Gibbs and Cav went through the drawers.

"Lots of file folders, but I can't read the tabs," Becca said handling them by the edges. Pulled one out, opened it. "Russian. Everything is in Russian." Shook her head. "Shouldn't be a surprise. And better than code, I guess." Rethought that. "Unless it's Russian code."

"Laptop too. Looks like Russian," Jorge said. "Not passworded."

Cav's gut was twisting. Telling him to get moving, finish here. Go to Forest. Lori.

"Wait a minute." Gibbs pointed at the screen. "That is a map icon." He tapped it and a map popped up. Leaned over to look.

Becca, behind him, said, "That's the stash houses. The ones we're taking down today. Each one has an address and a hotlink."

Gibbs pushed one link opening a Word document.

"Russian." Cav groaned.

"I can read some Russian," Gibbs admitted. "Kind of a register. Seems to be a date for when they moved in. Names." He scrolled down. "Probably dealers. Dates. Quantity, price of sales, maybe. Both weight and dollars."

He scrolled down some more. "Look, two properties we didn't know about."

"Stop," Cav said. "That one." He pointed. "That name. The one crossed out. He was shot and killed in a drive-by last week. Can you print that list, those link pages? Email them to me? Send them to Dawson too. He'll want those two new properties."

"We don't have anything that ties Izzy or Grumpy to this operation. Only thing we have is Izzy owns the house and lets Grumpy keep a portrait here and use the desk," Gibbs said. "Nothing to hold them on. We could get a handwriting expert to look at the paper files. He could tell us who wrote them."

"Izzy is harboring a wanted criminal. That's enough to take them in for an interview anyway. Maybe get fingerprints. I want her phone records. We need to get to Forest," Cav said his gut roiling now.

"Try Stone," Gibbs said, and double clicked another map icon. "Routes. From Thailand through Mexico. Over the border. Three routes, dates. Uh, oh, shipment coming in today. Tomorrow."

"I want copies of that, too. Shit. Voicemail again. Where is everybody?" Cav couldn't stand here any longer. "I'm going over there. You coming?" he asked Ryan, and was surprised when Ryan nodded.

"I'll send this to DEA and call from the car about the shipment. You drive."

Cav gave Sally instructions and tried to listen as Gibbs contacted

DEA with the new information. Only half listened—because Lori was alone with a mob boss. He shook his head. Not alone. In a building with a few hundred other people. Might not even be in the same wing as Grumpy. Max and Stone were both there, too. But no one, NONE of them, was answering their phone. Where was Lori? Why wasn't she answering her phone? Max and Stone? For all he knew they were in bed together. Shit.

"I sent DEA the maps of the other two stash houses and the timeline for the shipment coming in," Gibbs said.

Cav nodded. Didn't really care. With the sirens on, he ran the red. Cut off two cars.

Chavez's voice came over the speaker. "Three squad cars are on the way to Forest. No sirens. I got a locksmith for the safe. And Mike is calling the college for Russian translators and a handwriting expert."

"We have translators," Gibbs said. "Be nice to be able to tie the books to either of those two women."

Cav sliced two minutes off the trip and cut the sirens two blocks out. He saw two squads already in front of Forest. A third pulled up to the parking lot entrance. They would attract attention, especially from bored residents. Hopefully Grumpy wouldn't be one of them. He wrenched his door open and jumped out heading for the building, but Gibbs blocked his way. Cav pushed him, but Gibbs caught him by both shoulders. "Stop. Think. You can't go storming in there."

Cav stepped back out of his reach and started around.

"Cav, stop!" Gibbs ordered. "Listen. We need a plan. If Lori is with the old lady, we need a plan."

"Dammit that's what I'm going to find out."

"How? You going to bust in there? And do what?"

"I'm going to tear her head off her shoulders if she touched Lori."

"Look at me," Gibbs ordered. "Look at me!"

Cav did. Blinked. Gibbs never raised his voice. Took a breath.

"Okay. Okay. I'm not busting in there, and I'm not tearing any heads off of shoulders." He turned around and leaned on the car roof. Thought of Lori. Laughing, smiling. Making love. Holding the ring. He turned back to Gibbs and was surprised to see Becca and Sally standing there watching him. He hadn't even heard them arrive. Tugged his hair.

Maybe not tearing heads off, right now. Not yet. "Okay." He looked at Sally. "Put your GoParty jacket back on. Tell the front desk you have a meeting with Lori. And Maxine Mansard. Find out where they are. Becca, you head for the rehab gym. Gibbs and I are heading for Max and Stone's rooms. Numbers 305 and 307."

Gibbs strode slightly ahead of Cav, both walking nonchalantly to the elevator.

"Yoo-hoo! Yoo-hoo! Guys? Over here," Lucinda sang from a chair in the entranceway.

Cav groaned. Not now.

"Ma'am," Gibbs said politely.

At the same time Cav muttered under his breath, "Not now." He pulled at Ryan's arm.

"Thirty seconds," Gibbs said. He turned politely to Lucinda. "How are you doing Ma'am?"

"I'm just fine. Went dancing last night." She giggled. Cav choked.

"Well," Gibbs said at a loss for words. Cav had told him about an old lady and dancing.

"In the ballroom, young man. We all danced. Of course, some of us continued in private. Like your two friends Max and Stone. They went back to his place." She giggled again.

"We're just on our way to visit them," Cav said, pulling at Gibbs.

"You're not going to catch them in the act," Lucinda said.

"Thank goodness," Cav muttered.

"How is that?" Gibbs asked.

"Not home. Neither one of them."

"Oh?"

"Went out after lunch. To the playhouse for the afternoon matinee, didn't they," she snorted. "Didn't invite me."

Cav looked around the room. Not sure what for. No one else was visible. Becca texted that the gym was empty. Sally texted, *No one here knows where Max or Lori is.*

Shit.

"Lori? Have you seen Lori?" Cav demanded.

"Oh, yes. Just a minute ago. Don't you know?"

"Where?" he asked looking around the room again, still empty.

Lucinda stuck her nose in the air and snorted. "That old Grumpy came by with her niece or whatever, met Lori, right over there." Pointed to the right. "Then they all went out into the parking lot." She nodded toward the back of the building. "Not two minutes ago. Didn't even give me the time of day."

His heart stopped. Lori. With a killer. Smiling Lori.

\*

Lori was so mad at herself she could kick something, preferably Grumpy who at this moment had one arm around Lori's waist and the other arm sticking a gun in her side. Or maybe Lori should kick herself, because she'd let Grumpy walk right up to her after Cav had said Lori should stay away from her. But Lori hadn't been paying attention. She'd accepted Forest's offer and was daydreaming about love and sex and her ring and going home to chill a bottle of champagne.

But she hadn't kicked anyone, at least not inside. She had to wait until they were outside. Away from the people in the lobby. Because when Grumpy had walked over and grabbed her in the hall she'd hissed, "Any noise and they die first. Then you." So Lori walked out to the parking lot with Grumpy and her niece.

The niece led the way dragging two heavy wheeled suitcases and a canvas bag and wasn't any happier than Lori. She stumbled and complained. "You can't leave me here. This is all your fault. Why are you taking all this stuff? You can buy new stuff when you get to Miami."

"Shut up and bring those cases. You're always complaining. This is your fault. I need to leave; the least you can do is carry my things."

"I did everything you told me. I shouldn't have to stay behind. There's room for me on the plane," Izzy whined.

"Shut up or I just might shoot you, too."

Too? Lori thought. Who else is she going to shoot? Then she answered her own question. Me, of course. The question is, does she shoot me before or after she gets on that plane?

The niece let go of the suitcases.

"Don't leave them there, you idiot. Move them to the curb."

Izzy gave Grumpy an ugly look and struggled to move the cases, dragging them three feet forward. Dropped them again. "Here's the limo now," she said.

Lori turned to look. Couldn't believe it. "A limo?" Lori said. "You're a fleeing felon and you're escaping in a limo?" A white stretch was turning into the lot. "And not just any limo, but a white SUV limo? Way to blend Grumpy."

Grumpy poked her hard with the gun. "Shut up. Make your snide remarks now, my little friend. You will pay for each one later."

"You won't get away with this you know."

"You think your brother and your boyfriend can stop us? Hah. They don't even know about us. And I'll be long gone in another hour." A burly man stepped out of the right passenger door of the SUV and Grumpy ordered him to load the suitcases.

Lori snickered. "I think the parking lot entrance is kind of blocked, Grumpy," she said and motioned her head toward the street where a squad car had stopped.

The niece wailed, "Cops? I told you we should leave right away, but you had to pack your things."

Grumpy mouthed what might be a curse in Russian and gestured with the gun to the burly guy. "Hurry."

Lori took advantage of Grumpy's distraction and kicked her in her kneecap. Not a hard kick because Grumpy held her too close, but enough to make Grumpy take a step to the side to catch her balance.

Lori twirled out of her grip. And away. Ducked behind the Forest van and ducked down.

"Stop her," Grumpy yelled at the man who pulled out a gun and fired. Twice.

"Don't shoot her, you idiot," Grumpy hollered. "The cops are here. Go get her. We need her alive."

The thug charged after Lori.

The squad car hit lights and siren and screamed into the lot.

Cav sprinted silently over to Grumpy while she was distracted, grabbed her gun arm and pushed down, and said quietly into her ear, "Police, Grumpy. Let go of the gun or I'll blow your fucking head off." See Gibbs? Not tearing off a head.

"She attacked me," Grumpy yelled. "That woman attacked me. I was only defending myself."

"Drop the gun. Or lose the head. Now."

Grumpy dropped the gun. "My bodyguard only went after her to stop her from attacking anyone else."

She'd sent her armed thug after a helpless unarmed woman. He really wanted to shoot her head off.

Gibbs arrived, picked up the gun, and grabbed Grumpy, nodding for Cav to go.

He raced after the thug who had disappeared behind the Forest van. Vaguely he heard another squad car screech to a stop. He slowed as he rounded the front of the bus and looked cautiously down the side. The hoodlum was at the back, his gun in one hand and an ugly smile on his face. He grabbed a struggling Lori out from where she was crouched. The thug yanked her arm, but she stubbornly clung to the bumper. He hit her in the face with his gun.

She screamed.

Cav charged.

The thug pulled his arm back to hit her again harder.

Cav couldn't get there in time to stop him.

Lori screamed again, twisted sideways. She let go of the bumper. Brought her free hand up and hit the goon hard in the throat, knuckles first.

He stopped. Choked. Reached for his neck. Gagging, he let her go.

Lori kicked him. Place-kicked him in the chin tipping him backward. He fell, both hands holding his throat as he retched and made strangling sounds.

Cav skidded to a stop, kicked the gun away from the thug. Pulled Lori into his arms, wrapped her tight. Her head fit just under his chin, and he pressed her face into his shoulder. Waited for his heart to stop racing, his breathing to slow down.

Kept his weapon on the downed man. Guy might have another gun. Most likely did have a second weapon.

He felt her heart racing too. Their hearts seemed to be beating in rhythm. "It's okay. It's okay," he crooned not sure if he was comforting her or himself.

The trooper from the squad car ran over and rolled the goon on his stomach and cuffed him. The creep was still wheezing and gagging, and Cav half hoped no one would think to take him to the hospital.

The deputy frisked him and found the second weapon. Put both guns aside.

Lori was shaking now.

"It's okay baby. You're safe." Cav stroked a hand down her back. He couldn't bear it if she were crying.

She lifted her head and pushed out of the comfort of his arms. She wasn't crying. She was laughing. "I got him. Did you see? Did you see? Did you see me knuckle him in the throat? Did you? Did you?"

She demonstrated and Cav whipped his head out of her reach. "And then I put him down with a heel to his face. Teach him to hit me." She turned to the man still on the ground. "Teach you to hit an unarmed woman. Creep." She was on a roll. "Bully. Showed you."

She turned back to Cav. "I did it. I put him down." She pumped her left arm up in a power sign. "I got him. Me." She pranced around in a circle punching both arms in the air, knuckles up, singing, "I got him. I got him."

The troopers watched, smirked. Cav didn't understand until the kid pointed to his own shoulder. Body cam.

Christ, he had taped the whole thing. And the cam was still running. Focused on Lori's victory dance. Cav jerked his head. "Get him out of here," he said as two more deputies came in to help. "Get him to a doctor." And he moved to block the three body cams.

Lori was still giggling. "I never really tried that. But I watched ML and Becca practice it. Wing Chun Kuen. A quick debilitating jab. I did it. First the jab." She punched the air. "Then the kick." She kicked up.

Cav couldn't find words, just watched. Her cheek was bleeding down her face and onto her blouse. He wished he'd kicked the goon himself. Twice. Hard. He tried to pull Lori in, but she was still celebrating.

"He made me so mad. I was mad already that I let Grumpy grab me. But then your squad car came by and I kicked her and ran. Maybe I was a little scared when he came after me, but he made me so mad when he hit me, I let him have it. Got him good." She jabbed the air again.

She stopped.

"I didn't kill him, did I? I wouldn't want to have killed him. Cav? Tell me I didn't kill him."

Cav wished she had. "No. You hit him hard enough to stop him. My men will take him to the hospital and get him checked out. I want you to go too."

"No."

"Yes." He reached over and wiped the blood from her cheek. Showed it to her.

Her eyes widened. "I'm bleeding? Argh. I'll hit him again. Where is he?"

Cav laughed. He couldn't help himself, and this time he did pull her in and hold her. She tried to back off and he said, "Give me a minute. This is for me. I need this." And they stood holding each other.

He finally pushed her away. He didn't want to, but he had to. This time she stood, calm. He nodded once. Coming down. "I have to go back to work. You need to go to the hospital, have a doctor look at your head."

"I'm fine," she said.

"Yes, you are," he said with a smile. "But—"

She interrupted him.

"Nurse Osimo is on duty today, I'll have her look at it."

"No. You need to be checked by a doctor for the official report."

"What official report?"

"The one which describes your kidnapping and assault."

"Kidnapping? Oh my gosh." She grimaced. "Okay."

"Can you talk?"

"What do you mean can I talk? I am talking."

"About what happened with Grumpy," he said.

She looked puzzled. "Why wouldn't I be able to talk about it?"

Because most women would be suffering from hysteria. But not his Lori. Well, maybe she had been a little hysterical. He was smart enough not to say that. "What happened?"

"Grumpy got me in the lobby. Walked right up and stuck her gun in my side. I'm sorry. I was distracted because I signed with Forest." She stopped. "No. Truth. I was thinking about you. Us. Last night. This morning. The ring." She held out her hand. Touched the ring. "Yes, distracted is the right word. Grumpy said she'd shoot everyone in the room if I didn't walk out with her, so I did. Her limo came in, and that—" she motioned with her chin to the creep in the squad car, "—creep got out. Then when I got a chance, when your squad car came into the parking lot, I kicked Grumpy in the knee and ran behind the Forest bus. He came and hit me, grabbed me. You saw the rest." She finished with a bright smile and jabbed her fist up in the air.

Yup. He had. He wanted to jab a fist in the air, too.

Grumpy and Izzy were cuffed and taken to the station where they were put in separate cells. After they were searched. The old lady had a second gun in her purse.

"Do you know where they were going? How they were getting there?'

"They were not going anywhere. She was leaving Izzy here. Plane somewhere. Private I think because Izzy said there was room for her. Didn't want to be left behind."

"Good. Sometime today, or if you're not feeling up to it, tomorrow, you'll need to come in and make a statement."

"Today. As soon as I get done with the doctor. Let me just tell them inside I won't be back."

"Okay. Becca will go with you. And take you to the station."

"No. I can drive to the station."

"I'll drive," Becca said walking up, dangling keys. "And you can tell me what happened here."

Lori smiled. "Cool. Us girls. Wait til you hear. I used Wing Chun Kuen. Wait til I tell you."

Becca yelled, "Oh my god. What's that?"

Lori spun around. Cav too, reaching for his weapon. Nothing there.

"On your finger, Lori. What's that on your finger?"

Cav chuckled and left them to their girl talk. He needed to interrogate prisoners.

He began with Izzy. She started talking as soon as he walked in the room. She didn't want an attorney or a deal. She was happy to share everything.

"I hate her. I hate her. I got out of that life. Broke away. Married John. They killed him. They pulled me back in. Kept me close. Made me clean and cook when the household staff wasn't there. That was my home they burned down. Mine."

She knew everything. Where the bodies were buried, both figuratively and literally.

Izzy wasn't the only one singing like a canary. The thug who had hit Lori would be hoarse for a week or two, but that didn't stop him from writing down everything he knew about the Russians. He wanted a deal not to be deported.

Lori had a bandage on her head. No concussion. Photos had been forwarded from the hospital. After she gave her statement to Sally, Jones came in and high-fived her. "Way to go, Sis. That was some neck jab. The kick was excellent."

"You saw? You saw me knuckle him?" Lori asked.

"Me and half the country."

"What do you mean? What do you mean half the country?"

"Online. Cop cam video got leaked, went viral online. Everyone wanted to see the hot chick take down a giant with a karate chop."

"Video?" she looked around at Cav then back to Jones. "What video?"

"Stu, the Deputy. His body cam. He caught the whole thing. Someone leaked it and it's gone viral. It's all over the web."

Her color drained. "Oh no."

Becca reassured her as she came in with coffee. "Not the kissing, hugging part. Or the celebratory dance. That part wasn't leaked."

"I'm all over the web? That's kind of embarrassing."

"Can't see much of your face and the blood kind of hides your features. But I'd say anyone who tries to hit you is in for a very rough recuperation for a few weeks."

# SUNDAY

Max served them all coffee and then gave Cav a plate with two warm apple fritters.

"I think I love you," he said as the aroma hit his eyes.

"From the looks of that ring, I think it's Lori you love," Mrs. Tubalt said.

Cav looked at Lori and smiled inside. Yeah, it was Lori he loved.

"We're both happy for you," Stone said.

We're? Cav thought. Yes. We're. Max and Stone were a team. "Thank you," he said. "And before we get into a discussion about wedding plans, none have been made."

He took a bite and lost his train of thought for a moment. Then, reluctantly, he put the sweet down and picked up his coffee to keep his hands busy.

"I want the three of you to know what happened to your properties. Firsthand. Not the garbled version you'll hear on the news. My involvement began when the three of you discussed selling your homes over dinner with Lori last week. She knew the blue house, your house Max, was not vacant. She and I, we drive by that house fairly often. So she drove to your home, Mrs. Tubalt and observed vehicle traffic in and out. Then she went to your farm Stone. Nothing overt there, but the place looked abandoned, not maintained by a property manager. She heard air conditioning. She brought her concerns to me while protecting your privacy. She only told me addresses. I took a look.

"Max, your place first. Mrs. Weldon's nephew, Donny, rented your house to his boss, Jeffrey Newton, a home builder. Newton needed a temporary place for a nice young couple with a baby whose occupancy permit was delayed. Donny had the keys to your house and lied to the contractor and his aunt. I've spoken with Newton, and I think you can deal with him directly, work something out. I don't think my office needs to get involved, unless you want us to."

"I think you're right. Give me all the information, and I'll give him a call. And I want to see my house."

Cav handed her a file. "But we are keeping your car. Donny used it to rob a few check cashing shops."

"My puddle jumper?" she said. "He used that car for a robbery. Whatever was he thinking? Not about a fast getaway."

"Truly, I think the only intelligent idea that guy ever had was renting your house," Cav said.

He savored another bite. "Stone, you and Mrs. Tubalt, you were both victims of a Russian drug trafficking ring. Mrs. Tubalt, your home was used as a distribution center for drugs." He turned to Stone. "Stone, your barn was used to manufacture and distribute black market pills containing heroin, fentanyl, and methamphetamine. The mob hired a couple of PhDs in chemistry, to make the drugs which were then supplied to places like yours Mrs. Tubalt."

They had heard most of this on the news, so it wasn't a complete surprise.

"A joint task force made up of DEA along with FBI, state, county, and city police was set up to deal with the drug ring. And based on what they observed at your house, Mrs. Tubalt, they raided multiple sites in a five-state area yesterday. About one hundred and twenty people were arrested, upper- and mid-level dealers, street level dealers. Buyers, guards, and enforcers. The task force confiscated drugs, guns, rifles, counterfeit currency."

"Wow. My house? It was responsible for yesterday's news?"

"Yes. DEA will be in your place for a few days, but it's in pretty good condition. DEA Agent Dawson will be contacting you with more information and a timeline for when you will be able to go back." He passed her Dawson's card and drank some coffee. Really good coffee. Maybe Max could teach Lori. No, he loved Lori's coffee.

"Stone, Federal HAZMAT teams are cleaning your property. They won't be releasing it for a few weeks. I haven't been inside, but they tell me there is some damage." He handed Stone a card. "If DEA doesn't contact you today, let me know, and I'll give them a reminder."

"How did these drug people know our places were empty?" Stone asked.

"Grumpy is the boss of the drug ring. She learned the same way you and Max learned about vacant properties. Gossip. She hung around the common areas and eavesdropped. Sometimes asked questions, what seemed like innocent questions. Like who was your property manager? She heard you tell someone about Stewards; she got his address and sacked him."

Stone shook his head. "So an innocent conversation gave her all the information she needed."

"Right. DEA has her in custody. For now, she's not saying anything. Claims she only speaks Russian."

Max snorted. "She spoke English here. Accented, but she spoke and understood fine."

"We know that. DEA has Russian interpreters, but she wants a Russian attorney. Her nephew, the man we call Brouska, is in DEA custody. He speaks English, too. The two have frequent conversations in Russian – with our interpreter in the room. FBI has his partner, a guy named Eggert, who is wanted for killing two FBI agents. Plus, we can tie him to a number of drug related killings. Including Izzy's husband."

"What happened here yesterday? Gossip is saying there was a shootout in the parking lot. Did that have anything to do with the drugs?" Max asked.

"Another reason I wanted this meeting," Cav said taking a moment to get two more bites of the fritter while it was still warm. Sipped some coffee, all three watching him.

"Izzy fell in love. Went straight. Moved out on her own. She changed her name to Burke, to further distance herself. She bought her own home. Married John Smith. Shortly after, he turned up dead in an alley. Now according to Izzy, after Smith was killed, Grumpy made her sign her house over to the old lady who turned it into a stash house and forced Izzy to move back into the family home.

"Grumpy sold the family mansion to Izzy for a dollar so Izzy's name would appear on the deed for county records. But she made Izzy sign a quitclaim, deeding the mansion back to Grumpy. At the same time, she made Izzy sign her house over to Grumpy. We found all the deeds in Grumpy's office files. So the county records look like Izzy owns Grumpy' s house and Grumpy owns Izzy's. A little complicated but it worked for her and confused law enforcement. She burned down Izzy's house so she would have no place to go."

Stone said, "No surprise Izzy wants to bury Grumpy."

"Why burn Izzy's house?" Max asked.

"Grumpy misunderstood her doctor. She thought she had to move out of Forest. She didn't want to. She wanted to stay at Forest, mainly because she had easy access to vacant properties. Lori's brother discovered that staff at the nursing home knew ahead of time when patients would be transferred from the hospital and talked freely. All Grumpy had to do was sit around and listen. That's what the fight was about. Izzy wanted to keep her house. Grumpy had it burned."

"But Forest doesn't kick people out," Lori said.

"Right. But she didn't know that then. It wasn't until later that Grumpy realized Forest wouldn't make her move out."

"Okay, but what happened in the parking lot?" Max asked again. "You still haven't told us."

"Grumpy grabbed Lori. Threatened to shoot everyone in the lounge if Lori didn't go with her." It still infuriated him.

"Oh, you poor dear," Max said and grabbed Lori's hand. "What happened?" she asked Cav.

Cav laughed. "You need to see what happened. I sent you each a video. It's not to be shared. Though part of it has leaked online."

Now he was done and could eat while they watched. Each time he saw it he was torn between terror and pride.

"You did good. I'm proud of you," Max told Lori, giggling and watched it again.

Cav stood. "We need to be going."

Stone shook his hand. "Thank you both. This is an amazing story. No hurry with the clean-up at my farm. I'm not moving back. I'm selling. I'll put the proceeds in trust for my granddaughter. Max is selling too." He smiled at her.

Cav told Max, "Let me know when it goes on the market. We'll be looking for a place, and we both like your blue house." He didn't know if they could afford the blue house, but two incomes? Maybe.

"It isn't going on the market," she said.

"What? Someone already bought it?"

Max's turn to smile. "Why, the two of you of course. We'll negotiate a deal that makes us all happy."

Cav smiled. He knew they would. "I think I love you too," he told her.

And, holding hands, Cav and Lori headed to Kevin's for Sunday family dinner.

jay gee heath has enjoyed a fun cornucopia of careers. She began as a teacher, shifted to the National Park Service, prepared tax returns as an Enrolled Agent, and retired as an adjunct professor teaching computer applications. She is a voracious reader and her husband nagged her for years to write a book. Right Talents was her futile attempt to prove him wrong. Now she is hooked on writing and Right Solution is her most recent mystery.

Email the author at jaygeeheath@gmail.com

Visit her webpage at http://www.jaygeeheath.com/

www.ingramcontent.com/pod-product-compliance
Lightning Source LLC
Chambersburg PA
CBHW070303120726
47910CB00007B/2354